Samuel Ives Curtiss

Franz Delitzsch

A Memorial Tribute

Samuel Ives Curtiss

Franz Delitzsch
A Memorial Tribute

ISBN/EAN: 9783743409859

Manufactured in Europe, USA, Canada, Australia, Japa

Cover: Foto ©Raphael Reischuk / pixelio.de

Manufactured and distributed by brebook publishing software
(www.brebook.com)

Samuel Ives Curtiss

Franz Delitzsch

FRANZ DELITZSCH.

FRANZ DELITZSCH:

A Memorial Tribute.

BY

SAMUEL IVES CURTISS,

PROFESSOR IN CHICAGO THEOLOGICAL SEMINARY.

EDINBURGH:

T. & T. CLARK, 38 GEORGE STREET.

1891.

PRINTED BY MORRISON AND GIBB,

FOR

T. & T. CLARK, EDINBURGH.

LONDON, ... HAMILTON, ADAMS, AND CO.

DUBLIN, ... GEORGE HERBERT.

NEW YORK, ... SCRIBNER AND WELFORD.

PREFACE.

———o———

This Memorial was undertaken at the suggestion of my friend, Professor Caspar René Gregory of the University of Leipzig. It is not designed, however, in any way to forestall a large work which is promised in German. As several years may elapse before that work can appear, it is hoped meanwhile that this little volume may be welcomed by those who knew and loved Professor Delitzsch.

It lays no claim to completeness, although it is based on an intimate acquaintance with him which began in 1873 ; on a careful examination of original documents, not previously brought to light : and on personal interviews with those who were acquainted with Professor Delitzsch and his mother for years, one of whom was an old schoolmate at the Nicolai Gymnasium.

While it does not contain his correspondence, and many details which would be so interesting to former pupils, it may perhaps present some pictures which may be helpful in giving at least a faint conception of the noble personality which we associate with the name Franz Delitzsch.

If all our theologians could be animated with his spirit, debatable questions in theology would be discussed without bitterness, and childlike faith would be combined with scientific research.

No effort has been made to suppress anything concerning his early difficulties and struggles. The whole story is told so far as it is known to me. I can only believe that the more his life is studied the greater must be our admiration for his industry, his learning, his self-denying labours, and for his warm devotion to the cause of Christ.

SAMUEL IVES CURTISS.

CHICAGO, *February* 1891.

CONTENTS.

———o———

APPENDIX.

FRANZ DELITZSCH.

—o—

CHAPTER I.

SKETCH OF DELITZSCH'S LIFE.

"Remember: 'The kingdom of heaven suffereth violence, and the violent take it by force.'"—DELITZSCH.

THE family, whose name Franz Delitzsch inherited, was a very humble one. The name, however, as appears from the records, was Dölitzsch. The father, who was born in Leisnig, a town beautifully situated on the road from Leipzig to Dresden, was a dealer in second-hand clothes. The grandfather, who was a grenadier in a regiment under the command of Major-General Lecoq, came from Wendisch Luppa,[1] a small place in Saxony, near Oschatz.

His mother, whose maiden name was Müller, was from Schkeuditz, a town near Leipzig, on the road to Halle. Young Dölitzsch was married quietly on the 1st of June 1803, when he was a little over

---

[1] The figures in the text refer to the notes at the end of the chapters.

A

twenty years of age. It is clear from the church records, which I have examined with greatest care, that both of the families represented in this marriage were of pure German extraction, without any trace of Jewish blood, as has sometimes been imagined. So far as we can learn, there was no fruit of this union until about ten years later, as will soon appear.

Some years ago Professor Delitzsch wrote regarding a discovery made by his colleague, Professor Kahnis, of a Magister Andreas Delitzsch, who was connected with the University of Leipzig in the time of the Reformation. In this article Professor Delitzsch says that for nearly ten years he, too, was known as Magister Delitzsch, and seems to wish that in some way a connection might be established between him and the one whose name was thus exhumed from oblivion. With evident regret, however, he remarks that probably there is no connection between the family of Dölitzsch and that of Delitzsch, on account of the different spelling of the name.[2] But the spelling proves nothing, for down to the present century the spelling of names often differs according to the sound, and the sound according to provincial varieties of pronunciation. Thus we find in duplicate records of the baptism of Delitzsch's father, that in the official record kept by the sexton the name is written Dölitzsch,[3] while in the copy kept by the superintendent of the parish the name is Delitzsch, and in the record of the marriage of his parents at Schkeuditz the name is also written Delitzsch.[4]

No nobility of family, however, could add anything to the lustre of his name. All who may hereafter bear it might well wish to prove that in some way their families were connected with his.

He first saw the light in a house which was then No. 1299 Grimmasche Steinweg, a continuation of Grimmasche Strasse, outside of the ancient city limits, February 23rd, 1813. On the 4th of March immediately following, according to the universal custom of the Lutheran Church at that time of allowing but little delay between birth and baptism, he was baptized in the Nicolai Church.

It was a humble company which gathered around this babe, who was to be one of the brightest theological lights of this century. The Mayor of Leipzig and the Rector of the University might well have been his godfathers, and Superintendent Rosenmüller[5] might have counted it an honour to have baptized such a child. But as the world did not know what his future would be, he was baptized by Magister Rüdel, a sub-diaconus of the Nicolai Church; and those who were present, according to the church records, were as follows: "his father, Johann Gottfried Dölitzsch, second-hand dealer; his mother, Johanna Rosina Müller: the godparents were, Friedrich August Schlegel, journeyman stockingmaker; Maria Sophia, an aunt or cousin from his mother's native place in Schkeuditz, daughter of a deceased shoemaker; and Franz Julius Hirsch, second-hand dealer," after whom he seems to have been named, and who was doubtless the intimate Jewish friend of the family whom he mentions so gratefully in his Autobiography as Hirsch Levy,[6] and with whom, as I have learned from a grand-nephew[7] of Hirsch Levy, the family had their home.[8]

They lived for years in the third storey of a rear tenement in Prussian Lane (Preuss. Gässchen), which was then No. 24, now No. 11. The front house bears the date of Aō 1711. The tenement consisted of three small rooms, facing on a court about 26 feet by 12.

If our supposition be correct with reference to the one last named in the record of this baptism, Jew[9] as well as Christian was represented.

Certainly no Christian godfather could have been more mindful of his obligation, nor more beloved by his godchild,[10] than was Hirsch Levy, who, late in life, at the age of seventy-eight, two years before his death, publicly acknowledged the Messiah whom he had long recognised in secret, and was baptized as Theodor Hirsch. Some may be inclined to question whether it would be possible for a Jew under any circumstances to be a godfather at a baptism in a Lutheran church. Doubtless such a case could hardly occur now; but at a time when Leipzig was thoroughly poisoned by Rationalism, as at the beginning of the present century, we may well believe that baptisms were performed in a rather perfunctory way. The parish was very large, including several thousand people. It is very unlikely that the sub-diaconus could know more than was indicated on the slip of paper[11] which contained good Christian names. Or, if he happened to know " the second-hand dealer," he might choose to interpose no barrier to his pre-sence. It must be remembered, too, that at this time the Jews, who had no civil rights, were driven to all sorts of subterfuges when they desired to enjoy cer-tain privileges among Christians. It is therefore easily conceivable that Hirsch Levy in his intercourse with Christians, when it seemed necessary, assumed the name which we find on the record of baptism, Franz Julius Hirsch, dropping his last name, Levy, as he did many years afterwards at his own baptism ; and this seems the more probable, since after the most careful search the name Franz Julius Hirsch is not to be found in any civil or church list of Leipzig, although on the baptismal record of the child Dö-litzsch he is indicated as a resident of the city, and as engaged in the same occupation as that followed by Hirsch Levy. Besides, the name Hirsch Levy had been long on the list of those Jews who, while not citizens, enjoyed the protection of Leipzig, because it was the place of their birth.[12]

We may well believe that while young Delitzsch was an infant, close observers could see the promise of a remarkable career. His mother told a friend, still living,[13] that as she was standing at the door of her house with her babe on her arm, during those

days which were so fateful for Napoleon in connection with the battle of Leipzig, a soldier who was
passing stopped, and, putting his hand on the little
boy's head, said, "Mamma, mamma, this child will
one day be a great man."

Concerning his boyhood we have very few particulars. Although he speaks of his childhood as a
hard one, he was nevertheless a merry, exceedingly
lively lad, and so zealous in gymnastics, that he
dangerously injured one of his eyes.[14] It is not
improbable that in the stall, which was kept alter-
nately by "Uncle" Hirsch and his mother, and which
was much patronised by the university students, he
found abundant inspiration, and that here the foundation was laid for his literary career.

He first studied in a boys' school, then in the free
city school, of which Plato was director and Dolz
vice-director.[15] Here, under these leading spirits, he
says that he became a complete Rationalist.[16] In
1827 he entered the Nicolai Gymnasium, of which
Dr. Nobbe was rector, and continued his studies
until his graduation in 1831. He must have won
a high rank as a scholar. Professor Dr. G. A.
Winter, a librarian of the University of Leipzig,
who was a member of one of the lower classes, says
it was a current report among his mates that at the
final examination Delitzsch spoke Greek fluently
with one of the examiners, Professor Grossmann,[17]
who had a great reputation for scholarly attainments. Whether this was an exaggeration or not,

the younger students evidently considered him extraordinary.[18]   At a centennial celebration in connection with the Gymnasium, he was one of the seven
pupils appointed to represent the institution.   On
this occasion he delivered an ode.   At his graduation, on the 23rd of September 1831, he presented
a farewell poem ; and in the programme which was
issued by the rector, and which contains poetical
memorials by former pupils, young Delitzsch receives
special recognition, as the following quotation shows :[19]
" Instead of giving many other specimens, the following poems by a pupil just graduating, Franz Jul.
Delitzsch, are inserted, in which he gives a proof of
the old experience that classical culture, in pro-
portion to its thoroughness, is of advantage in the
cultivation of our own tongue.   He has happily
combined modern classic authors with ancient, and
has chosen Hölty as a model of the former."   While
previous graduates who secure recognition have one
poem each in the programme, Delitzsch has five.[20]
We give some of the stanzas of the last poem without
translation.   Those who are acquainted with German
will notice the significance of the final stanza.

DER MOND.[21]

Wenn das Spätroth hingesunken,
Und der stille Abendstern,
Immer goldner, wie ein Funken,
Strahlt aus düsterblauer Fern'
Sieht es silbern durch den Wald
Und mit tausend kleinen Sternen
Ist das Gezweige darin bemalt.

.   .   .   .   .

Dank ihm, der mit mildem Glänzen
Dich, O Luna, dort erhöht.
Der die Welt in Reigentänzen
Um die grosse Axe dreht ;
Der sich Diademe flicht,
Aus des Blitzes goldnen Strahlen
Und aus des Abends Rosenlicht.

Ihr, der nimmer dich veralten
Und so nah uns glänzen lässt,
Dass du uns von seinem Walten
Wunderhold erzähltest ;
Hast auch jüngst in voller Pracht
Traut vom Ewigen gesprochen,
In des Johannes heilger Nacht.

.   .   .   .   .

O gleich deinem Untergange
Doch dereinst mein Sängertod !
Sanft erbleicht dir Aug' und Wange
Vor der Sonne Morgenroth.
Heil, wenn mir am Sterbetage
Vor der Auferstehungsonne
Sanft, so wie dir, das Auge brach!

According to the last page of the programme
which I have mentioned, young Delitzsch was one
of those who were proposing to study theology.
Speaking of that time, however, he says that he
felt himself drawn to God, but that the person of
Jesus Christ was veiled in utter darkness. He went
to the university in the Winter Semester of 1831–
32 to study philosophy and philology. While seeking for truth he became absorbed in the systems of
the great German philosophers, and was especially
attracted by the idealism of Fichte.[22]

But at length a great change came over him. A
gifted, pious fellow-student, named Schütz,[23] who was

an intimate friend, had long laboured for his conversion.   One day as he was near the old Grimma
gate he became a new creature in Christ.

As Zöckler relates: [24] Under the guidance of this
friend his spiritual life was deepened by the study
of the older devotional literature of the Lutheran
Church by such mystical works as Arndt's *Wahren
Christentum* and Rieger's *Herzpostille*.   Among other
works he mentions particularly one of a pietistic
character by Nedderesn, *Empfindungen und Erfahr-
ungen im Christentum*, of which he said that " it
never ceased to be his dearest *vade mecum*."   Besides, he mentions the benefit which he received
from the writings of two Austrian Roman Catholics,
from the religious philosopher Anton Günther, and
his pupil Pabst.   He was especially and permanently
influenced by studying the works of Jacob Böhme.

While his new Christian experience made a complete revolution in his life, the catalogue of the
university does not indicate that he ever changed
from the department of philology to that of theology,
but it is said that he read theology privately with
men of like mind.[25]   There can be no doubt that
from this time on Franz Delitzsch was a changed
man.   He brought forth the fruits of the Spirit.
He was kind and tender - hearted ; and while he
could be just as a critic, he never returned railing
for railing, although he had ample opportunity to
do so in the Review of which he was editor-in-chief.[26]
Christian love was certainly the ruling passion of his

life. In the society of kindred spirits, who subsequently became eminent as leaders of the Sacramental Host, among whom was Ferdinand Walther, afterwards of the Missouri Synod, he passed the last three years of his university course (1832–34), which he says were the most beautiful of his life.[27] He was a leader of a little circle which met weekly for mutual edification from 1835 to 1842. Out of these little meetings grew his *Communion Book*,[28] which passed through seven editions, and was richly blessed, so that Professor Luthardt remarked at his funeral, that perhaps he had more joy in the knowledge that this book had been a blessing to many souls than in the fame which had come from all his learned works.[29]

In the year 1835, on the 3rd of March, when he was still in his twenty-second year, he became doctor of philosophy. The dissertation does not seem to be in existence, although in his *Vita*, which has been preserved, we have some account of his studies.[30]

During the following year a sore trial came in the death of his father, who had the reputation, among those who knew him, of having been a dissipated man. Delitzsch simply tells us that he died in his arms on the night of the 4th of April 1836, at the age of fifty-four. From other sources it is reported that he was entirely out of sympathy with the life and aims of his son, whose presence even was not agreeable to him, so that young Delitzsch was often compelled to withdraw to his own room. After his decease his son mourned exceedingly for a long time, because he feared his father had died without hope; but he was finally comforted by a dream in which he appeared to him, and told him that his prayers in his behalf had been answered.[31]

He had already chosen the Old Testament department. He laid a foundation in Hebrew at the Nicolai Gymnasium,[32] and began his study of Rabbinical Hebrew with the Jewish missionary Becker,[33] who was in the habit of attending the fairs at Leipzig, where many Jews were wont to congregate.

In after years he never allowed an opportunity to pass to perfect himself in the knowledge of Rabinnical Hebrew and of the cognate languages. His thirst for knowledge was extraordinary. He was first a pupil and then an intimate friend of the famous Arabic scholar, Professor Fleischer, until the death of the latter in 1888. Von Orelli relates that after Delitzsch returned from Erlangen to Leipzig, when he was fifty-four years of age, he attended Fleischer's Society with the students. He told Professor Gregory that he also took Arabic lessons of the American missionary, Dr. Eli Smith, and said that he owed more to him in that language than to any one else. He was for years on intimate terms with the Jewish missionary, Dr. J. R. J. Biesenthal, with Dr. Baer, and many others. Like the busy bee, he gathered honey from every flower, and stored it away in his hive.

Young Delitzsch spent seven years in quiet study,

until in 1842 he became a licentiate of theology
and a *privat-docent*, with the privilege of lecturing in
the university.

In the catalogue of the University of Leipzig for
the Summer Semester, M[agister] F. Delitzsch, theological licentiate, is advertised to give an exposition
of the prophecies of Isaiah.[34]   In 1834 he was
made a *professor extraordinarius.*   Meanwhile, he
was called as a regular professor to Königsberg ; but
he declined, because he was a strict Lutheran, and
Königsberg combined the Lutheran and Reformed
Confessions in what is known as the Union.

In 1846 he was called to the University of
Rostock.   Meanwhile, on the 27th of April 1845,
he had married Miss Clara Silber, the only daughter
of a wealthy family whose three brothers, one
after another, had died of consumption.   Professor Delitzsch's first famulus, Bernhard Caspari,
is authority for the statement that Miss Silber found
her future husband by the bedside of her brothers,
to whom the young professor was much attached,
and whom he visited in a pastoral way.   He himself
says that he became acquainted with her through
the religious meetings of which he was leader.   Not
only her brothers, but also her mother, were converted through his instrumentality.

For information concerning his activity at Rostock, I am indebted to Professor Eduard König.   While
there he was still engaged in laying broad foundations.
When we remember that it was his habit from one

end of the year to the other to rise at five o'clock, and that he regarded the ordinary vacation as a waste of time, and that work was his meat and drink, we can understand that those were fruitful years, and are not surprised at the variety offered in his courses of lectures, including elements of Syriac, Arabic, Samaritan, and Persian.[35]

Nor was his activity confined to the preparation of learned lectures and the pursuit of Semitic studies. He had a part in founding a Home for the rescue of abandoned children. Professor König writes that a series of documents which he wrote as secretary still give testimony to the zeal which he developed in this branch of service.

In 1850 he was called to Erlangen, where he laboured seventeen years, with kindred spirits like Hofmann, Thomasius, and others, in happy and useful activity. Here, as in Leipzig, he made himself felt in Christian work. He was accustomed to gather the children together every Sunday evening during several years for a children's service. These meetings were attended by the parents of the children, as well as by university students.

On the 7th of December 1857 his beloved mother died in his arms in the seventy-fifth year of her age. At the death of his father, as he was still a student, he was not able to support her. She therefore engaged as before in the sale of second-hand books jointly with the old family friend Hirsch Levy, in a stall at No. 2 Neumarkt Strasse, on the west side

of the street, at the corner of Grimmasche. This
business she continued after the death of his foster-
father. Many a university student raised his hands
in surprise when, on inquiring the price of some
book by Professor Delitzsch, he learned that the
famous professor was her son. This condition of
things, as he says in his Autobiography, pained him
exceedingly, but all entreaties were in vain. He
was seen at different times, on his visits to Leipzig,
tenderly to embrace her on the street, and was heard
to call her his dear, good mother, and to beg her in
the most moving way to go with him. While she pre-
ferred to be independent, he joyfully contributed to
her support. He gives her the testimonial that she
was respected and beloved by all who knew her; and
in this all the old citizens heartily join. He writes,
" She was a faithful cross-bearer, to whom the words
Luke vii. 47 may well be applied." He said, " She
had little pleasure in this world, and was glad to go
home." Her grave is in the old Johannis Churchyard in Leipzig.[36]

For seventeen years Professor Delitzsch continued
at Erlangen. He seemed to have become rooted to
the place. He had become endeared to all at the
university, which he had helped to raise to a high
tide of popularity, and which was drawing students
from various foreign lands, including Greeks, Scots-
men, and Americans. It did not seem likely, as he had
declined several calls to other places, that he would ever
leave this field where he had become so renowned.

But Professor Luthardt, who was then Dean of the Theological Faculty at Leipzig, had determined to make an effort to secure Delitzsch. Kahnis heartily approved of the plan, but was faint-hearted. There were two serious difficulties in the way of obtaining him. The Faculty at Erlangen were determined to keep him; the Theological Faculty at Leipzig, with the exceptions already mentioned, were either indifferent or, because they regarded him as too strongly Lutheran, opposed to his coming. The well-known Old Testament critic, Tuch, who was in declining health, said, if he came at all, he should come over his corpse. But Luthardt, with the aid of Kahnis in the Faculty, and with Tischendorf using all his influence with Von Falkenstein, the Saxon Minister of Worship, carried his point.

The Theological Faculty of Erlangan were exceedingly sore over the matter, and never really forgave Luthardt for robbing them of their brightest jewel. Luthardt, however, had told them that if they lost Delitzsch, they could get an Evangelical man to fill his place; but if he failed to win him for Leipzig, it would be impossible to get a man in sympathy with himself and Kahnis to take the chair made vacant by Anger's death, that is, Delitzsch's fame as a scholar and writer would secure a place for him at the University of Leipzig which would not be open to a man with the same religious opinions but less distinguished. It was a proud day for Luthardt and Kahnis when he came. These three, who were

then in their prime, formed an incomparably attractive centre for theological study.

But in the midst of great successes he had great
sorrows.   He was compelled, after the close of the
Franco-Prussian war, January 17th, 1872, to part
with his second son, who had served as assistant-
surgeon, but who was not able, through his untimely
death, to become a member of the Medical Faculty at
the University of Leipzig, as he proposed.

Although he had the joy of seeing his first son,
Johannes, who gave great promise as a theologian,
become a *professor extraordinarius* in the university,
and the husband of the beautiful and accomplished
Johanna, daughter of Dr. Baur, his joy was soon
turned into profound grief by the decline and death
of this son at Rapallo in Italy, February 3rd, 1876.
I shall never forget the pathos with which he read
for me, when we first met after this sad event,
David's lamentation over Saul and Jonathan.

But he gathered strength and hope, and had
comfort in his son Hermann, who is in a banking
house, and in his youngest son, Friedrich, born September 3rd, 1850, who had become famous for his
contributions to the department of Assyriology.   He
was cheered on his seventieth birthday by many
congratulations and good wishes which were sent
him, not a few of which came from foreign lands.
He wrote, "And they sounded so sweetly in my
ear; as sweetly as the cradle hymn sung to the child
when it is rocked to sleep."   He carried on his work

with freshness and vigour after he reached the age of seventy; and it seemed as if he might be spared as long as his colleagues Fleischer [37] and Drobisch.[38]

He had always been a lover of flowers. They spoke to him the language of Heaven and of God's love.[39] He delighted in their beauty and their perfume. He was rarely seen in his study, on the street, or in the lecture - room without a rose, a bouquet, or, at least, a little nosegay. The students often laid flowers on his desk.

As he went to Holland to make a special study of the yellow hyacinth, he forgot that he was over seventy-five years old, and indulged in a bath in the North Sea, which, although he afterwards somewhat recovered his strength, was the remote occasion of his death. He was able to lecture the last half of the Winter Semester 1888–89 and during the summer of 1889, but at the close of the year's work, in connection with the visit to the baths at Ilmenau in Thuringia, which it was hoped would tone up his system for the work of the following year, he was attacked with a paralysis of the lower limbs, which was so serious that he was carried in a chair to the train, and from the train to his bed in his own home, from which he was destined never to rise.

Here, humbly awaiting God's will, he was tenderly nursed by his devoted wife, who was constantly by him. In the full possession of his intellectual faculties, bolstered up in bed, he was still able through the aid of Pastor Wilhelm Faber, whom he

loved like an own son, to follow the doings of the
Institutum Judaicum and the publication of the
Messianic Prophecies; and through Lic. Theol. Dr.
Dalman, upon whom the choice had fallen to issue
the eleventh edition of his Hebrew New Testament,
he was enabled to make some contributions to that
which he desired should be a permanent form of
the text.   When he could not work he was cheered
by the singing of a canary and the presence of a
pet dog which lay on his bed.

His friends remembered him daily with flowers,
the reception of which he was glad to acknowledge
when he could.[40]   On his birthday, February 23rd,
so many were sent that his room was almost trans-
formed into a flower-garden.   His entire family were
gathered around him, including children and grandchildren.[41]

He gradually failed, until the morning of the 4th
of March, the anniversary of his baptism, when the
end came.   At the usual morning devotions, when
his sons were present, as he was unable to read, his
wife read for him, with sobs, a passage concerning
the resurrection.   His lips moved in an inaudible
prayer, and finally he said, " I am weary, and will
go to sleep." [42]   These were his last words.   Turning
his face, he sweetly fell asleep in Jesus.

Death was no surprise to him, he had been ready
for years.   He once wrote a friend, in reply to congratulations, something as follows: " I thank you:
my attitude of mind is that of waiting for the signal

which calls me to the eternal morning." At another time he said, " With Christians everything should be consecrated, eating and drinking, sleeping and resting, but you are not to look to me [for a model]. I do not represent it, although I ought to."

It is the testimony of several sextons that it was often his custom on passing an open church, even on a week-day, to go in for a season of devotion.

The following prayer, which appeared at the end of an article published by Professor Delitzsch on the incarnation of God,[43] only two months before his death, might well have been his last, just before his spirit left this world :—[44]

"Lord JESUS help us through the Spirit of promise to recognise Thee and Thy Father whose name is in Thee, and in faith to embrace Thee, and to love Thee, although we do not see Thee with the eyes of sense. How else could we return to God in our separation from Him except through Thee ? 'Thou art the way.' How could we be delivered from the pain of doubt, and the instability of human opinion, except as we hold on to the word of God through Thy divine mouth ? 'Thou art the truth.' And how could we joyfully go into death if Thy pierced body were not, as it were, the rent veil of the other world ? 'Thou art the life.' Thou hast overcome death and Hades. Thou hast opened heaven for us. We kiss in spirit the marks of the nails in Thy body pierced for us, and cast ourselves at Thy feet which were fastened to the cross for us, and pray to Thee as the incarnate Love who hast shed Thy blood for us, and cry with Thomas, treading all doubting thoughts beneath our feet, 'My Lord and my God.'"

NOTES.

[1] He was born in Wendisch Luppa, June 21st, 1756, and was baptized the next day with the name Gottfried. As the name Johann does not appear in the register, he must have assumed it afterwards.

[2] *Saat auf Hoffnung*, 1885, p. 86.

[3] Johann Gottfried Dölitzsch was born April 19th, 1783, in Leisnig (not Leipzig), and was baptized on the 21st of the same month.

[4] I have a certified copy of the marriage certificate, and have also carefully examined the original.

[5] Johann George Rosenmüller (born December 18th, 1736; died March 14th, 1815) was then superintendent and pastor of the Thomas Church, and was also professor of theology. He is not to be confounded with his son, Ernst Carl Friedrich Rosenmüller (born December 10th, 1768; died September 17th, 1835), under whom Professor Delitzsch afterwards studied.

[6] See Delitzsch's *Vita* and Autobiography in the Appendix.

[7] M. Gustav Meyer, a gentleman who knew Professor Delitzsch intimately for years, and who remembers his granduncle well, whose real name was Hirsch. He was called indifferently Hirsch Levy or Levy Hirsch, although in the old directory of the city his name appears as Hirsch Levy.

[8] The following is a description of the tenement in which the family lived. The first room after reaching the landing was $6\frac{1}{2} \times 6\frac{1}{2}$ feet; the next, the family room, which was $10\frac{1}{2} \times 11\frac{1}{2}$ feet; and opening out of this was a dark chamber $12\frac{1}{2} \times 13$ feet.

[9] M. Meyer has no doubt, from his knowledge of

his granduncle's relation to his family, that he was present at the baptism.

[10] Young Delitzsch, according to M. Meyer, was accustomed to call him "Uncle Hirsch."

[11] The original slip of paper from which the record was entered into the church-book is still in existence, and, as is customary, is kept on file. It, too, has been carefully examined in connection with the preparation of this sketch. The names of the godparents are written in pencil.

[12] According to the records of the city, Hirsch Levy was born in Leipzig 1776. He was known as a "Schütz-Jude." He dealt in second-hand books, as has been stated. He died May 24th, 1845, and was buried in the old Johannis churchyard. On his tombstone, which has disappeared, stood this inscription: "Lord, now lettest Thou Thy servant depart in peace, for mine eyes have seen Thy salvation." In the notice of his death in the *Leipziger Tageblatt*, Leipzig, May 1845, No. 152, p. 1566, he is erroneously called a citizen; but the description given of Theodor Hirsch corresponds entirely with that of Hirsch Levy, who disappeared with the appearance of Theodor Hirsch.

[13] Amanuensis C. F. A. Rothe of the University Library.

[14] See von Orelli's article in *Der Kirchenfreund*, Basel 1890, p. 98.

[15] This school is not to be confounded with the Nicolai Gymnasium, as has been done by some writers.

[16] *Saat auf Hoffnung*, Leipzig 1890, p. 148. It is an error when Prof. Dr. A. Köhler, in the *Neue Kirchliche Zeitschrift*, Leipzig 1890, p. 235, speaks of Plato as director, and of Dolz as vice-director, of the Nicolai Schule.

[17] Superintendent, professor of theology, and pastor of the Thomas Church (born November 9th, 1783; died June 29th, 1857).

[18] His marks, as furnished by the kindness of Prof. Dr. Adelbert Gebhardt of the Nicolai Gym-

nasium, indicate that at first his standing was not
high.   Young Delitzsch entered the third class in the
Gymnasium, and ranked twenty-sixth among thirty-
three class-mates.   The rector has left on record the
following remark: "That information concerning him
is still too indefinite to form a judgment, but that he
is certainly promising."   In 1828 he was the twenty-
second in the second class, numbering twenty-eight.
In 1829 he was the twelfth.   During the first part of
1830 he was the twentieth in the first class, and in
the last half of the same year the fourteenth.   In
1831, when he graduated, there were none that had a
higher rank than himself, except one that was better
in Hebrew.   In conduct he was not quite perfect.   In
Hebrew and mathematics his marks were 2 = good,
in the other branches 1 = very good.

[19] See Programm, etc., p. 38.

[20] The titles are as follows: 1. "Als mein Finke
gestorben war im März." 2. "Ad aviculas." 3. "Hoel-
teii mortem praesagientis carmen Latine redditum."
4. "In somnum." 5. "Der Mond."

[21] Programm, p. 40.

[22] *Panegyrici magistri*, Lips. 1826–50: "Quam in
Academiam discessisset Richteri scholis ad philosophiam excitatus, Fichtii idealismus amplexus est."

[23] Zöckler says, in the *Daheim*, vol. xxvi. p. 436,
that this Schütz, who became a teacher, is neither to
be confounded with the philologist Christian Gottfried Schütz, nor with his son, Carl Julius Schütz.

[24] "Zur Errinerung an Franz Delitzsch," in the
Daheim, vol. xxvi. pp. 436–438.

[25] Köhler, in his article on "Franz Delitzsch,"
Neue Kirchliche Zeitschrift, Erlangen und Leipzig,
1890, p. 236, says: "Vor allen auf die Förderung und
Vertiefung seines inneren Lebens bedacht, trat er in
einer Kreis gleichgesinnter Kommilitonen ein, darun-
ter der nachmalige Führer der lutherischen Synode
von Missouri Ferd. Walther, ferner Bürger, Brohm,
Löber, Fürbringer Geier, Schiefedecker u. a., welche

später ebenfalls Pastoren in der lutherischen Kirche Nordamerikas wurden. Mit ihnen studierte er die h. Schrift, die dogmatischen und asketischen Schriften der lutherischen Kirche, und versenkte sich so immer tiefer in ihre Anschauungen und ihr Bekenntniss."

[26] He was editor in chief of the *Zeitschrift für die gesammte lutherische Theologie und Kirche*, 1863–1878, and was associated and had a part in the book reviews from 1843.

[27] Since writing the above I have received von Orelli's article on Dr. Franz Delitzsch in *Der Kirchenfreund*, Basel 1890, pp. 97, 98: "Was mir der theurer Lehrer vor 23 Jahren unter sein Bild geschrieben hat: 'die Liebe hört nimmer auf, so doch die Weissagungen aufhören werden und die Sprachen aufhören werden und die Wissenschaft aufhören wird'—das steht mit Fug und Recht unter seinem Bildniss." Köhler says of him: "Sein ganzer Sinn war auf Helfen, Heilen, Fördern gerichtet."

[28] *Saat auf Hoffnung*, Leipzig 1890, p. 150.

[29] *Ibid.* p. 141.

[30] See his *Vita*. It is interesting to know that Fürst is reported finally to have said to Delitzsch: "I cannot teach you anything more; you know as much as I do."

[31] This was reported to Amanuensis C. F. A. Rothe of the University Library by Delitzsch's mother.

[32] As Dr. W. H. Ward of *The Independent* suggests: we might be inclined to suppose that Delitzsch first learned Hebrew from his Jewish friend; and this is possible, although he mentions the Nicolai Gymnasium as the place where he acquired the rudiments.

[33] The first treatise which he read in Rabbinical Hebrew was *Or leeth ereb*, "Light at Evening."

[34] His courses of lectures at Leipzig before he removed to Rostock were as follows: Summer semester, 1842, Isaiah, four times a week: Winter semester, 1842–43, Psalms, four times; grammatical interpretation of Habakkuk, once: Summer, 1843, Psalms, twice; Zephaniah, with grammar, once: Winter semester,

1843–44, Genesis, four times : Summer semester, 1844,
Hebrew grammar, based on Zephaniah, twice : Winter
semester, 1844–45, Psalms, twice ; Leidens- und Aufer-
stehungs - Geschichte Jesu, twice : Summer, 1845,
Nahum, once ; Philosophie der Offenbarung oder
Grundlinien der speculativen Dogmatik, twice : Winter
semester, 1845–46, Erklärungen, der Psalmen, von
Ps. xlii. an mit vorausgeschickten Prolegomena in den
Psalter, three times ; Disputatorium zur Besprechung
kirchlicher Zeitfragen, twice.

[35] He began in the Old Testament department
with Genesis and Zephaniah: then followed through
the rest of his activity at Rostock, Messianic Psalms ;
first part of Isaiah ; second part, five hours a week
(later four hours) ; Job, five times ; introduction to
the Old Testament, four times, extending through two
semesters ; Psalms of Asaph and Korah ; selected
passages from Jeremiah and Ezekiel ; history of the
prophets and of the prophetic writings, six times ;
Song of Songs, twice. During every semester he
lectured on the New Testament five times a week—
Hebrews, Romans, Matthew, John, Galatians, and
James. He also lectured on the Oriental languages
as indicated above, and, one semester, "de notionis
organici et organismorum usu theologico." Moreover,
he conducted every semester exegetical exercises.

[36] The following is a translation of the inscription
on the headstone: " Under this grave-stone rests in
God Frau Johanna Rosina Delitzsch, died on the 7th
of December 1857 : Luke vii. 47, Rev. vii. 17." At
her funeral her son requested that only passages of
Scripture should be read.

[37] Fleischer, the celebrated Arabic scholar, died
1888, at the age of eighty-seven, and retained his
mental vigour and power to teach almost to the last.

[38] Drobisch was born 1802, is still living, although
he does not lecture any longer.

[39] He once said he smelt the love of God in the
flowers ; and more beautifully still he remarks in the

preface of his *Iris:* "Mit dem Blumen stand ich stehts auf vertrautem Fusse, sie erzählten mir himmlischen Dinge in ihrem Dufte fühle ich die Nähe und den Odem des Schöpfers."

[40] The following is a copy of a postal card sent to Prof. Dr. Gregory in acknowledgment of a "Christ rose." It was written in a strange hand, but signed by himself:—

"LEIPZIG d., 26*ten Dec.* 1889.

"Verehrter, geliebter College und Freund: Was für ein Prachtstück der Treibhaus Flora haben Sie ausgesphät um es als symbolischen Fest-gruss zuzusenden. Haben Sie Dank für diesen neuen Beweis Ihrer treuer Freundschaft. Ich begrüsse wie auch meine Frau Ihre Frau Gemahlin herzlichst.

Freundschaftlich,
Ihr
mich leidlich befindender Delitzsch."

[41] I am indebted for these particulars to Lic. Theol. Dr. Dalman.

[42] Compare with this end of life the wish expressed in the last stanza of his poem, entitled, *Der Mond*, p. 8.

The following lines are taken from the album of a friend. They bear the date of April 7th, 1846:—

"Thrice blessed is the soul, to whom
Jesus has come with His salvation,
Christ with His anointing,
The Son of God with His glory.
In remembrance of your friend
In the one faith, which
Is the source of all comfort
and of all joy.

Fr. Delitzsch,
ord. Prof. and Dr. of Theol. at Rostock."

[43] *Die Menschwerdung Gottes, Saat auf Hoffnung,* Leipzig 1890, pp. 4–13.
[44] *Ibid.* pp. 12, 13.

CHAPTER II.

"In meines Herzens Grunde
Dein Nam' und Kreuz allein
Funkelt all Zeit und Stunde;
Drauf kann ich frölich sein."

THE funeral was held in the Pauliner Kirche, or the University Church, of Leipzig, Saturday, March 8th, at two o'clock P.M. It was literally attended by Jews and Greeks, as well as by the ordinary Christian audience. After a voluntary on the organ and a funeral hymn by the University Choral Society, a hymn was sung by the congregation, which had been selected by the deceased:—

Valet will ich dir geben
Du arge, falsche Welt;
Dein sündlich böses Leben
Durchaus mir nicht gefällt.
Im Himmel ist gut wohnen,
Hinauf steht mein Begier;
Da wird Gott herrlich lohnen
Dem, der ihm dient allhier.

Rat mir nach deinem Herzen,
O Jesu, Gottes Sohn!
Soll ich ja dulden Schmerzen,
Hilf mir, Herr Christ, davon;

26

Verkürz mir alles Leiden,
Stärk meinen blöden Mut;
Lass selig mich abscheiden,
Setz mich in dein Erbgut!

In meines Herzens Grunde
Dein Nam' und Kreuz allein
Funkelt all Zeit und Stunde;
Drauf kann ich frölich sein.
Erschien mir in dem Bilde
Zum Trost in meiner Not,
Wie du dich, Herr so milde
Geblutet hast zu Tod!

The addresses which follow were delivered by
his pastor and confessor, Rev. F. G. Tranzschel, by
Professor Luthardt in behalf of the Theological
Faculty, and by Count Eckstädt in behalf of the
Evangelical Lutheran Central Society for Missions
among Israel.

ADDRESS BY THE REV. F. G. TRANZSCHEL, PASTOR OF THE JOHANNIS KIRCHE IN LEIPZIG.

"There remaineth therefore a rest to the people of God."   Amen.

Beloved mourners : dear sympathising Church,—In
this fatal winter—now, too, this sacrifice!—one of
the most painful which the Church militant yields to
the Church triumphant. Many shining names have
paled in the last moons in the heaven of the Church
—genuine standard-bearers of the banner of the
cross of our Lord Jesus Christ in a time of great
world commotions. A feeling of loneliness must
take possession of an army engaged in conflict
when one leader after another falls. Now, too, this

star has set.   Beaming in the first magnitude, and
yet twinkling so mildly, he has shone over almost
half a hemisphere, not only in the academic circle
as an ornament of German learning, but also in the
Church; not only in the Lutheran Church of the
German nation, but far beyond the sea, even to
England and America.   The most prominent theologians of the various Churches of Great Britain
have been among his most enthusiastic pupils and
admirers.   Indeed, not only in the Christian, but
also in the Jewish world the name of Delitzsch has
shone.   For he was at home in the literature of the
Rabbis as none other among the living, and perhaps
as none before him.   We may well say, The truest
friend of Israel is dead.   A great man has fallen in
Israel, although he was small of stature.

If we would speak of the blessing with which the
Lord graciously crowned this long life, so rich in
activity, we must make use of the words of the
Book of Job, which the dear departed one was
inclined to consider the greatest book in the Old
Testament (xxix. 19 ff.): "My seed sprang up by
the water, and the dew remained upon my harvest.
My glory was continually renewed in me, and my
bow improved in my hand.   They listened to me
and were silent, and waited for my counsel.   When
I came to their affairs I was compelled to take the
chief seat, and dwelt as a king among his servants,
since I comforted the mourners.   I was a father of
the poor, and rejoiced the heart of the widow." [1]

There are thousands who have been secretly aided by him with rare generosity. His pupils also are to be reckoned by thousands, who have fed upon his mental gifts, who all bless the memory of this righteous one. With a broad sweep this sower of the Church has cast noble seed. That which he sowed was not merely " Sown in hope." [2] Many an acre planted by him he has seen become green, although in after years. Even he himself has already been permitted to reap where he had sown. But now, in a good old age, he has come to the grave like a shock of corn fully ripe.

Beloved mourners in the Lord,—Before I alluded to your affliction I spoke of the affliction of the Church. Were you not always accustomed [to find] in the case of the dear departed, that he belonged more to his work, to science, to the Church of his Lord and Saviour, than to his home? Above all, thou mourning widow, I know how many sacrifices of thy lonely hours are connected with the richly blessed work of the tireless professor! How many hours which were due thee from him hast thou spared him that the rich treasures of his knowledge might not remain ungathered! Those are women's sacrifices which are offered in secret, rewarded by the Lord alone,—sacrifices of unselfishness, full of understanding for the high calling and the rare gifts of the husband, such as only noble women's hearts are able to bring. But was not your living together for more than forty-five years all the more genuine, pure, and happy because it rested on such uncommon virtues? How thankful he always felt in thy debt—loving debtor! Even on his death-bed thy care was still most welcome to him. And how happy as a child, forgetful of his work, he could be, when he had once laid down his pen for days or weeks, and when you together could enjoy the times of recreation in the mountain, or on the sea, or on the beautiful Rhine. He, the man of the Old Testament, who often spoke in the language of the Old Testament, to whom it was a pleasure to put the present even in relation to the Old Testament, was nevertheless the man of the most manifold interests. Whatever was important in the domain of literature did not remain unknown to him. Whatever was "lovely, or sounded well, whether it was a virtue, whether it was a praise, he meditated upon it." He, a friend of flowers, like few, had beheld the lily of the field, as if he would follow the command of the Lord in the widest sense, not only with the eyes of the gardener who plants it, not only with the eyes of the child who plucks it, not only with the eyes of the naturalist who analyses it. No, he had woven a religion and a poetry in his learned understanding, as only a child of God can live in the domain of nature. And the last of all his labours, which he completed on his dying bed in his last days, had reference to the "yellow hyacinth," in order finally to find the golden yellow-flower and its history, with which Luther compared the colour of the red-yellow hyacinthine precious stone, which may have been shown him by his friend Spalatin in Altenburg. While earlier, blue hyacinth was the colour of the precious stone (sapphire), and of the flower (larkspur), Luther puts in place of it yellow, so that ninety-six passages in the Old Testament in the designation of colours must be changed.

What a mental inspiration the intercourse with such a rich spirit, even in domestic intercourse! What a happy time, when his household was not yet darkened with the shadow of death, that period of his life at Erlangen, when his house was a social centre for professors and students! But then he was tested like Job. He saw two sons sink into the grave before him, one Johannes, who was already professor of theology here in Leipzig; the other, Ernst, shortly before his promotion as a member of the Medical Faculty, after he had served as surgeon on the military staff sixteen months in the war against France 1870. Then came an hour of mourning for the father, when here in Leipzig he appeared before his students in the lecture-room with the sigh: "I am a poor man!" But God did not suffer him to become poor. The rich gifts of his spirit and heart remained intact. He was permitted to see the rich happiness of both his sons who are still living, and of his nine grandchildren. In all the relations of life in which he was placed, he showed himself the amiable, approachable man of learning, as the many-sided fine theologian, above all as the

living Christian by whom the care of his own soul
was considered as of the highest importance.   It is
true that the results of new investigations in the
Old Testament department, which was the scientific
domain to which he gave special attention, seemed
to bring about an overthrow of former views.   And
although this great departed Old Testament theologian
did not remain entirely uninfluenced by the changes
which the new period had made in the traditional
views, nevertheless he took his position as champion
of the faith of revelation with all the fire of his
spirit and with all the splendour of his scientific
attainments.   He recognised a deep gulf between
the old and the new theology.[3]   He saw himself
standing among the Old Testament scholars of our
day, solitary as a torso, as an old forester in a
vacant clearing.

But to his last breath he remained in his theology
a decided Lutheran, although without any narrow-
ness.   Not as if mere orthodoxy was of the highest
importance.   He insisted on spiritual life, on personal
Christianity, on personal fellowship with the Lord ;
not as if he had found in mere scientific work the
chief blessing for the kingdom of God.   He feared
that mere intellectualism without unction would
result from the development of theology in our day.
And how full of unction was the work of his life !
Even in the most exact scientific argumentation he
used a consecrated language, the deepest tones of his
believing heart were ever heard.   Yea, " when thou

art converted, strengthen thy brethren." Since that significant turning-point in his life in the third decade of this century, when he was converted from rationalism and entered into sympathy with a little circle of Lutherans, some of whom afterwards settled in America : how much the Evangelical Church of our age is indebted to him for strengthening its life of faith, from the time of his first love, when he was the crystallizing point here in Leipzig by sermons and devotional services for an *ecclesiola* which many still remember, to that incomputable catalogue of his writings, concerning which he declared that he himself could not make it complete ! But if he had not left the Church anything else than his *Communion Book*, with its mystical depth and spirituality, in which he embodied the best of his personality, thousands upon thousands who have taken this book as their guide to the altar would bless him for it. Yea, "strengthen thy brethren." "Strengthen the things which remain that are ready to die," is the text of this fast-day. That was the chief work of his life, the ideal aim of his spirit to awaken a dead people, to strengthen the dying in Israel. Every one among the Jews who sought, however feebly, to engage in a conflict of faith between life and death, turned to him.[4] His correspondence alone in this department required almost the full strength of a man. Here, indeed, he had assistance in the *Institutum Judaicum*, which was called into being by him. And the last joy of his life was that he could see the first sheet of the revised edition of his Hebrew Testament,—the final edition. After he had seen this sheet he read nothing more. His Hebrew New Testament was the most effective missionary among the Jews of the East. He was the soul of missions among Israel in all Christendom.

Can we think that the vacancy made by his death can ever be filled ? God gave him a rare power of work; even at the age of seventy-seven for the greater part of the year he rose before the sun. The dawn found this industrious, youthful old man at his work. He had no other conception of life than that of work. Indeed, he could not conceive of the rest which remaineth for the people of God above in light, without work, without activity for the glory of God, without progress from one splendour to another. As he spoke to me once concerning his end, when he was still in health, he gave expression to the hope that God would preserve him from a time of weakness, when he should be compelled to be inactive. And God granted the suppliant his request. To seventy-seven years of health He added only half a year of sickness. Indeed, even on his sick-bed He gave him strength so that he could prepare writings for the press, little leaves which he jestingly called "white and blue butterflies." He was even able to examine some candidates who sat about his bed. It is true that he had to experience the patience of Job. The conclusion of his life was the time of the Passion. But he endured it humbly and patiently.

God gave him a little strength, he said to me finally, but God will also be satisfied with this small degree of strength. And from the passage with which I blessed his end he singled out, "There remaineth, therefore, a rest to the people of God." In many a letter by him which I had occasion to read, he wrote at the close, in view of his great age, "You will soon see old Delitzsch no more, but at the throne of the Lamb we shall meet again." Now he is there in green pastures and by fresh waters, whither the longing of his soul was directed. Our Saxon Church celebrates its fast-day by his bier. *Kyrie eleison* resounds in the conflict of our days. Protect Thy lonely Church, O Lord, Thou Lord of great and small. Let us not be orphans! Let the sparks and the fire of Thy seven-armed candlestick not be extinguished among us! From Thee are all gifts. Thy Church is not founded upon men, but stands or falls with Thee alone, Lord Jesus, the Crucified and the Risen One, Thou Lord of the living and of the dead! It is well that this is our comfort! With this comfort we call after the dear departed, our *vale.* Farewell, thou fearless confessor of Jesus Christ, thou great master of science, thou splendid teacher and father of the Church, thou good Samaritan to Israel, thou fatherly friend, thou humble child of God. "There remaineth, therefore, a rest to the people of God." We plant thee in the winter field as noble seed of an eternal spring! "Sown in hope!" Amen.

In behalf of the Theological Faculty, as the senior
member of it, and as a friend of our departed
colleague for many years, I am to dedicate a word of
remembrance here at his bier, and to call after him
our last farewell. Blow on blow, loss on loss have
befallen our Faculty during the last years, as have
scarcely ever befallen a Faculty in such frequency
and in so short a time. To Wold, Schmidt, Kahnis,
Lechler, and Baur, Franz Delitzsch is now added as
the fifth, our ornament and our boast; for none of
us, beyond his own special department, embraced so
wide a circuit of manifold learning, and through the
splendour of his name carried the reputation of our
Faculty so widely beyond the sea as he.

Here in Leipzig, his home, he began his scientific
course at our university, and here he ended it,
after he had belonged to Rostock and Erlangen in
the intermediate period beyond 1846 and 1867.
Awakened in his youth to religious belief, and de-
cidedly inclined to the Confession of the Lutheran
Church, he undertook all his work in the service of
the Church, and in making a religious impression on
hearts. It was, perhaps, a greater joy to him that
his *Communion Book* was instrumental in blessing
many souls than the fame of his entire literary
career.

In the first period of his scientific activity fell the movement which was opened in the treatment of the Scriptures by Hofmann of Erlangen in his epoch-making work, *Prediction and Fulfilment,* in the beginning of the fourth decade of this century, whose views many of us who were then young theologians greeted and received as a gospel of freedom. Franz Delitzsch's learning trod the path here indicated in an independent and helpful activity, and thus were produced the rich blossoms and fruits which he yielded in his theological lectures to his pupils, and in a series of scientific works of a systematic and especially of an exegetical sort, to the scientific world as well as to the members of the clergy.

That movement came to an end through the lively interest which was directed to the critical questions concerning the Old Testament, and which since then has chiefly moved the mind and heart. Working without rest, and keeping himself open to all questions of his department, he did not decline to enter upon these questions of literary and historical criticism. In the course of time he gradually modified his earlier position in many ways. But none could be farther than he from finding in the Holy Scriptures only an object of critical or in general of merely scientific investigation. They were always to him the sacred source of Divine revelation, which he approached with pious reverence, and in which he at all times found the nourishment of his soul and a fruitful source of meditation. He always sought to imbue the hearts of his scholars with this feeling.

Although his industry was so untiring from early morning, and although we must exceedingly admire him, and recognise in him a man of comprehensive learning, the thing which should be most emphasised regarding him was his power as a teacher, and his personal relations to his pupils which none, perhaps, had cultivated with more sincere sympathy than he. Nothing gave him greater pleasure than to know that his pupils were pursuing good courses, and nothing caused him more pain than to see a deviation from the right way, and perhaps an estrangement and coldness on the part of his scholars. He shared with them of his fulness without grudging, and devoted himself with self-sacrifice to their work in the examination and correction of their exercises. He not only served those who were nearest him in a self-sacrificing way, but he also enlarged his circle, and for many years gathered young Englishmen and Americans about him once a week for scientific discussion.

While such an activity extended itself through the Christian Church, both that which was near and remote, there was connected with it, at the same time, the effort to serve the non-Christian Israel in a missionary way, which went like a scarlet thread through his entire life. He offered the greatest sacrifices of time and strength in this service, and no unpleasant experience could make him err from it.

He devoted the work of a lifetime to the translation of the New Testament, as well as to its revision and correction.

And so I could continue to speak for a long time of his rich and tireless work, which did not even end with old age, and which was always seeking to learn, as a model for us all. But if in that which I have hitherto said some things may perhaps be less known to one or the other of his colleagues, nevertheless all knew him who were associated with him as the modest man of learning, and as the most amiable of colleagues, whom none could dislike, and with whom nobody could be displeased, but whom all must love as the fine-strung man, possessed of tender feelings and genuine sympathies, who found it hard in the business of his office to suffer his personal sympathies to give way to the cold business aspects of the affair; and, not to omit this, not the least as the friend of flowers, who was not often seen without a flower in his hand, upon the street or upon the platform. Flowers and colours were not only the darlings of his heart, but also at the same time the objects of thorough study. This interest for a flower, the yellow hyacinth, is connected with his death. It led him to Holland and Haarlem, and on that occasion he allowed himself to be enticed into taking that unwise bath in the cold North Sea which resulted in a serious illness; and although its evil consequences were transiently removed, it probably laid the germ of his death, which seemed to be so far away from his otherwise sound constitution. On his sick-bed he was still occupied with that flower, and dedicated to it a treatise which, apart from the revision of his Hebrew New Testament, and apart from a preface to his book on the *Messianic Prophecies*, in which he sought to embody the fruit of his theological work in the Old Testament department, was the last which he wrote or dictated. The last completed advanced sheet of the *Messianic Prophecies* was laid on his bed the day before he died. Only the end of his life ended the unwearied work of this man.

So he was ours, and as such he was taken from us, from our university, our Faculty, our Church and theology, the scientific world, and the Christian world in general—and I may perhaps be permitted to add, he was also taken from me, since I was closely bound with him for years, and with Kahnis, who went home before him. Now they have both left me. When our university, when our Theological Faculty, mourning, lays its palms upon his bier, and when the Theological Faculty of Erlangen, to which he belonged seventeen years in most fruitful activity, unites with us,—this is the only thing which remains for us in order to honour and thank him. But how little that is in comparison with what we are indebted to him! Never will his memory and the gratitude to him in our hearts be extinguished; and our theological youth, as we hope, will take pains, in grateful devotion to his memory, to learn from him and imitate his example. Thus we take leave of him, leave of thee, beloved friend and colleague. *Have pia anima! Requiescas in pace et lux perpetua luceat tibi! Have atque vale!*

ADDRESS OF COUNT VITZTHUM VON ECKSTAEDT, IN THE NAME OF THE EVANGELICAL LUTHERAN CENTRAL SOCIETY FOR MISSIONS AMONG ISRAEL.

In deep affliction and genuine mourning, the Evangelical Lutheran Central Society for Missions among Israel, as an external sign of its hearty thankfulness and admiring recognition, lays a garland on the bier of the beloved departed one whom the Lord has taken from us.

It was Franz Delitzsch who founded this Society twenty-two years ago, with two friends who have gone on before him into eternity,—Plitt and von Erdmannsdorf,—with the earnest desire that through a united activity they might see more members from the people of the Old Covenant led to our Lord and Saviour Jesus Christ.

Besides, he united with it other similar societies in Germany and outside of Germany, as the Norwegian and the Bavarian Societies for spreading Christianity among the Jews. This latter Society was founded by him in 1863 in Erlangen, and the Saxon Chief Missionary Society, whose Jewish missionary he was destined to be in 1839, and to whose committee he belonged until his death. With the origin of the Bavarian Society in 1863 he began the publication of the magazine *Saat auf Hoffnung* (Sown in Hope), which last January began its twenty-seventh year, adorned with his name. Delitzsch, however, with his heart full of burning love for Jesus, was the creative and propelling power of the work which was thus begun. He never relinquished his first love. All the while more glowing, it burned with an enthusiasm and a manifold activity which mocked old age. Through it he won and warmed by means of the *Instituta Judaica*, which have been revived since 1880, and through the Missionary Seminary, friends, and youthful pupils, and co-workers. His love was not mere feeling. It ripened into permanent fruit.

In the clear persuasion which rested upon the Lutheran Confession, "Only God's word does it," he placed his masterly command of the Hebrew language at the service of a translation of the New Testament into Hebrew. By means of this translation, which has attained a circulation of more than 60,000 copies, Delitzsch put an instrument into the hands of the Jewish Mission which, as the hammer that dashes in pieces the heart like a rock, will never be blunted.

For this, the greatest work of his life, the Lutheran Church should never be wanting in thankfulness. This thankfulness many have already bestowed upon him, who, desirous of salvation, have read the New Testament, and who have turned to the Shepherd and Bishop of their souls. Here the thanks culminate which to-day we utter by his bier.

Attacked with mortal illness, he completed his last work, *Messianic Prophecies in Historical Succession*, which he expressly indicated as a legacy for the workers in the Jewish Mission. May it bear fruit!

Thus Franz Delitzsch has assured his memorial in the Jewish Mission and among the people of the Old Covenant.

Rest in peace, and may the everlasting light shine upon you!

At the conclusion of Count Vitzthum's address the following hymn was sung by the University Choral Society of Saint Paul's :—

> Wenn ich einmal soll scheiden,
> So scheide nicht von mir;
> Wenn ich den Tod soll leiden,
> So tritt du dann herfür.
> Wenn mirs am allerbängsten
> Wird um das Herze sein,
> So reiss mich aus den Aengsten
> Kraft deiner Angst und Pein.

The remains of this great master in Israel now repose in the South Churchyard of Leipzig, in the immediate neighbourhood of the place where Napoleon, in the year that Professor Delitzsch was born, saw his star going down at the battle of Leipzig. He awaits the morning when God's people, both Jews and Gentiles, shall be gathered together to meet their Lord.

NOTES.

[1] This passage is given according to Luther's version, cf. vers. 13 and 15.

[2] There is an allusion here to the magazine which was published by Professor Delitzsch in the interest of Jewish Missions, and which was called *Saat auf Hoffnung*.

[3] The reference here is probably to theology as represented by the school of Ritschl.

[4] The literal rendering is, "Wherever a flickering wick under the ashes of servitude to the law fought the conflict of faith between life and death, to him everything turned from the Jewish world."

CHAPTER III

"Womit kann ich Ihnen dienen?"—DELITZSCH.

DELITZSCH was an attractive lecturer from the very beginning. He possessed in an eminent degree the qualities which interest students— genius, enthusiasm, learning, freshness, and originality.

Whatever criticisms may be made regarding a lack of exact scientific method of presentation, he had that which is the most important characteristic of a great teacher—the power to inspire his pupils. This is of more value than the ability to beat into them certain dry details. Any pedagogue can do that. But if any man could take his hearers up to the third heavens and show them things which were unutterable, it was Delitzsch.

He prepared himself for his lectures as if it were the only work which he had to do. His pupil, Köhler, professor in Erlangen, tells us that his lectures were wrought out, in respect to style, with the greatest pains, and that he sought to attain the utmost finish.[1] But as Delitzsch himself assured me, they never became stereotyped. He was not like the once eminent American professor, who wondered why the students had ceased to enjoy his lectures, since they were the same which he had delivered for twenty - five years. Delitzsch loved new forms of expression; he was always acquiring new stores of knowledge, and it was his earnest desire to serve his students in the best way.

When he first began to lecture in Leipzig, in 1842, as a *privat-docent*, he had good audiences. His first famulus [2] relates that, when he reached the account of the Fall in Genesis, his room was crowded with law and medical students, who had come to hear what he had to say about Satan, and make sport of it. He was warned before he entered, and those who came to mock were not rewarded for their pains.

In 1873, I was informed that it was his custom to begin in one of the smaller lecture-rooms at the opening of the semester, but it was soon necessary to seek a larger room.

Until the last he had large audiences. This is certainly a remarkable testimony to his power, when we remember that Ewald, in his old age, could command only a "handful of auditors," [3] and that the brilliant Tholuck, in the last years of life, became such a mental wreck in his public efforts that he could not command more than ten students, and even they probably attended his exercises out of respect. [4] But no such melancholy spectacle greeted the eyes of his former students. "His bow abode in strength."

Count Baudissin has well said, that although opinions might be divided regarding his books and his lectures, there could be but one opinion regarding his intercourse with students.[5] It was charming. It was not only fatherly, but when one was alone with him it was even brotherly in its affectionateness.

Surely none who ever went to drink a cup of coffee with him at the Bonorand, or in any other place, could forget the delight and inspiration of his presence.

In the earlier days he is reported to have gone to the rooms of poor students to take them with him to get a cup of coffee. He often visited them in sickness, and is said at times to have taken useful remedies.[6] He was a physician of souls as well, a faithful and successful pastor, who knew how to speak to the heart with an eloquence born of the conviction of the truth of what he was saying, and of love for the soul which he was seeking to help.

The smile of welcome with which he greeted new students, the kindness with which he inquired about their homes, is never to be forgotten; and the kiss and embrace with which he sometimes welcomed those who were nearest him, must have sent a thrill to their hearts.

I may be perhaps pardoned for giving a few personal reminiscences. In the spring of 1873 I found myself in Germany, without having previously thought that I could pursue a course of study there. I was finally compelled to set out on a voyage of discovery, as I knew nothing of the merits of the respective German universities. I finally reached Leipzig, and called on Professor Delitzsch. When he learned the object of my errand, he said slowly in English, "Are you willing to study in Leipzig?" [7] My heart at once answered the question in the affirmative. After he had drawn me to Leipzig, all unconsciously to himself, he drew me to his department, and when I did not find teachers that suited me, amazed me by offering me his services. It was certainly not for the compensation, for that was very moderate. He took me with a very elementary knowledge of Hebrew, and coached me in grammar and in reading at sight. He was kindness and help-fulness itself, from the beginning to the end of my stay.

I am sure many could bear similar testimony to his wonderful kindness and condescension. The amount of work which he did for students in propos-ing themes for investigation, and in correcting their exercises, is beyond computation. It was enough largely to occupy the time of any ordinary man. Besides this, he was helpful to his students at a later stage. If any of them sought promotion in the philosophical or theological department, and came to him for advice, he at once became deeply interested in their success. He was sure to suggest some

theme to them, to examine their plan of investigation, and to revise their work.   After they had
secured his interest, they were like so many sons,
whose success he desired.   Standing by the side of
the young man at the high desk in his study, pen in
hand, he made changes and corrections, and while
his right hand was busy, his left might steal around
the neck of the one beside him in a way to remove
all fear of this great scholar.   It is certain that
many owe their promotion and place in life to his
self-sacrificing and kindly efforts in their behalf.

An amusing incident is told at his expense.   It
was first related to me by Kahnis years ago, who
said, "Delitzsch is altogether too kind-hearted."
He pleaded until he carried the day for the promotion of a man as licentiate of theology, whom the
Theological Faculty did not consider at all fitted for
a theological career.   In seeking recently a verifica-
tion of this story, it was added, that after Delitzsch
had gained his point, and made some changes in the
dissertation which rendered it more acceptable, the
author, instead of remembering his benefactor, afterwards dedicated it to the deceased predecessors of
Delitzsch in the Old and New Testament depart-
ments: *manibus Tuchii et Angeri.*

Doubtless he had pleasure, and sometimes received
suggestions from bright minds, but it seemed to be
quite as much of a pleasure to him to serve as to be
served.   He once said, that he had no time for calls
of ceremony.   He wanted either to do something

for some one else, or have them do something for him.

His kindness, as may be inferred, extended to all classes of students. Although he was a strict Lutheran, men of all confessions found an open heart and a sympathizing friend. To multitudes who were once within the circle of his influence, the world seems poorer for his absence.

He had no ambition to found any school. He did what is far better: he inspired many to noble aims in life, and to seek the highest success. If a full list could be prepared of those who have been under his instruction, or, at least, under his influence, it would be surprisingly large.[8] In the hearts of his pupils his memory is certainly secure.

It remains briefly to consider him as a Biblical theologian. He stood firm as a rock in his adherence to orthodox Lutheranism. In his views of the Old Testament, however, he seemed to undergo a great change in the last ten years of his life. But it is clear to any one who carefully examines his writings, and who is familiar with his critical principles, that the change between his former and his more recent views regarding the origin and structure of the Pentateuch and other critical questions, was not the result of a sudden impulse.

For years he contended for perfectly unbiassed investigation. His standpoint was always different from that of Professor Keil in this respect. Almost thirty-eight years [9] ago he admitted that there were, at least, two different sources in the Pentateuch. Evidently Stähelin's *Untersuchungen* made a deep impression on his mind. But he then hoped that conservative scholars would be able to prove the Mosaic character of the Pentateuch.[10]

He also maintained, and in this he differed radically from Drechsler and Stier, that Divine revelation was of a progressive character, that it was conditioned and limited by those for whom it was designed and through whom it was mediated. Hence, that we are not forced to take the New Testament interpretation as representing the thought of the ancient writers, or of the people to whom their writings were addressed. He contended strongly for the primary historical application,[11] although, at the same time, he believed, for example, that the first David in his doing and suffering was typical of the second David.

His views of the Pentateuch were for a long time, as is well known, moderate. He held, at the very beginning of his published opinions, that certain parts of the middle books were Mosaic in fact, and that all was Mosaic in spirit, since a man like Eleazar was author of the Priests' Code, and a man like Joshua of the Jehovistic portions, while he held that Moses was author of a larger or smaller part of Deuteronomy.[12]

This view was rather the result of one of his happy guesses than of any exact investigation. He arrived at his results usually rather through intuitions than through long painful processes, although he could make detailed investigations.

But the time came when there were two Delitzsches struggling with each other. Some who were nearest him had occasion to observe the conflict. It might seem as if there were an inner and an outer circle among his friends and pupils. To the inner circle there were hints of new views, the outer were none the wiser. To a superficial observer he perhaps at times seemed vacillating.

Few have been called upon to pass through a more trying experience. To put the Torah on the critical dissecting-table gave him almost as much pain as Abraham felt when he bound his son to the altar. His religious nature rebelled against the process. It was not so much that he feared the inconsistency of change, as that he feared the effect of these views. His spirit bowed with the deepest reverence before the Scriptures. To him they were like a sacred sanctuary. A flippant and half-profane criticism made him heart-sick. When he looked at the evidence which was presented by the critics he was borne to one side, and when his mind was occupied with the conclusions which were drawn by them he veered to the other. It was not weakness, for he could stand firmly when he felt sure of his ground; nor was it weariness because of the blows that fell upon him, those he could have endured until death. But he neither felt sure of the truth of these new positions, nor of the trustworthiness of his old opinions.

I had occasion to see the change that came over him. He was much impressed with the epoch-making book of Graf,[13] and the companion book of Kayser.[14] These books raised questions in his mind for which he sought solutions. He suggested various subjects for investigation to intimate and advanced pupils bearing on these questions. The results were not such as to enable him to breast the storm which broke upon him with the publication of Wellhausen's *Prolegomena*. He finally published his own investigations in Luthardt's *Zeitschrift*.[15] The result was not surprising to any one who knew his state of mind.

The conflict was over. It would be a great injustice to a great man to say that in this he was merely a follower, that he lacked critical insight, and that he gave way under the weight of advancing years. Undoubtedly his forte was not minute criticism; and yet, at the same time, he had a quick perception and a clear insight. Without changing his principles one whit regarding free investigation which he had held for years, he adopted the new theories regarding the origin of the Pentateuch because he deemed them to be true.

I saw both sides in this struggle. Speaking of an interpretation which he had set forth in Isaiah, he said substantially, " The Church is exceedingly sensitive in regard to these matters. I have received a letter from a missionary in which he thinks the view that I have set forth [regarding a certain passage] is dangerous."

At another time he said to Professor Kautzsch, a former pupil of his, " You will have to change your views regarding the Pentateuch." He said to me in 1877, " If I were in your place, I would not put forth that theory as to the unity of the authorship of Isaiah." " But," I replied, " Professor, you defend that view." " Yes," he said, with emphasis, " I am an old man, but you are a young man." Afterwards some of his old pupils were surprised to find in his *Lectures on Messianic Prophecies*, which appeared in 1880,[16] indications of a change of views, especially concerning the authorship of Isa. xl.–lxvi. The change was made in all honesty and sincerity. It certainly was a remarkable spectacle, but entirely in harmony with the character of the man that, after he had reached the age of nearly threescore years and ten, he should have the courage to change his critical views. It came from an earnest desire to hold that which he deemed truest and best. But notwithstanding this great change in his views, he remained the same sweet, consistent Christian he had ever been.

NOTES.

[1] *Neue Kirchliche Zeitschrift*, Leipzig 1890, p. 241.

[2] Bernhard Caspari, a Jewish proselyte, brother of Professor C. P. Caspari of the University of Christiana.

[3] On the authority of Professor S. D. F. Salmond; see *The Expositor*, London 1886, p. 457.

[4] I have never seen a more melancholy example of a great mind in decay than when attending one of Professor Tholuck's lectures in 1873. Although he was still bright and instructive in conversation, he continually lost the thread of thought in his lecture. When I asked one of the students why he attended, he replied, "Out of respect for Professor Tholuck."

[5] *Theologische Literaturzeitung*, Leipzig 1890, col. 162.

[6] Von Orelli, *Der Kirchenfreund*, Basel 1890, pp. 103, 104: "Und wie erstaunt war so ein junges Studentlein wenn der ehwürdige Professor, der von seinen Unwohlsein gehört hatte, plötzlich in seiner 'Bude' erschien und ihm ein probates Mittel mit beredter Anpresung überreichte."

[7] He meant, "Wollen Sie," do you intend?

[8] The following is a partial list of his pupils who are professors in German universities:—Baudissin (Marburg), Buhl (Leipzig), Cornill (Königsberg), Ewald (Vienna), Gregory (Leipzig), Hommel (Munich), Kaftan (Berlin), Kautzsch (Halle), Klostermann (Kiel), König (Rostock), Köhler (Erlangen), Loofs (Halle), Mühlau (Dorpat), Orelli (Basel), Ryssel (Zurich), Schnedermann (Leipzig), Schürer (Giessen), Stade (Giessen), Strack (Berlin), Volck (Dorpat), Zahn (Leipzig), Zöckler (Greifswald).

To these may be added the names of the following Americans who are professors in theological seminaries:—Bissell (Hartford), Curtiss (Chicago), Gilbert (Chicago), Foster (Oberlin), Mitchell (Boston), Price (Morgan Park), Schodde (Columbus), Scott (Chicago), Smith (Lane), Welton (Toronto). These are a few of those whom I have been able to recall as his pupils. This list does not include those in England and Scotland who have studied under Delitzsch, nor those in Germany who have at least for some time come within the circle of his special influence, although they did not listen to his lectures.

[9] *Zeitschrift für die gesammte lutherische Theologie und Kirche,* Leipzig 1853, p. 544.

[10] *Ibid.,* Leipzig 1843, Part iv. pp. 145–147.

[11] *Ibid.,* Leipzig 1852, p. 271. 1. "It is erroneous that exegesis does not have to do with the meaning of the prophet, but with that of the Holy Spirit which caused these thoughts to be expressed in this definite form. . . . The meaning of the Holy Spirit which effects prophecy is absolutely the same as the person of the Holy Spirit Himself, and has in view, whether He makes use of Joel, or John, the author of the Revelation, as an instrument, nothing less than the entire contents of the eternal Divine decree and of its historical realisation in time and eternity. Through this absolute meaning of the Holy Spirit every prophecy has indeed an endless depth. Its first germ infolds within itself the entire tree of salvation, and the first lineaments are the sketch of the picture which history unrolls from one end in this life to the other end in the next. But are, therefore, germ and topmost twig, sketch and execution, identical ? Would there be a historical progress in prophecy and, in general, in revelation, if the Holy Spirit did not gradually reveal the limitless contents of His knowledge, comprising time and eternity, and did not communicate it in measure ? And in what way would it otherwise be possible than that He should enlighten human obscurity, not all at once, that only little by little He should remove human limitations, and should bring the relative character of human knowledge step by step nearer the absolute ? Prophecy is a divinely-wrought interpenetration of the divine and human, of that which is bounded and unbounded, of human short-sightedness which is not removed, and of divinely-mediated far-sightedness." . . .

2. "It is erroneous that the exegete should be under obligations to hold that as the direct meaning [of the Old Testament] without any further effort which the New derives from it." . . .

[12] See *Die Genesis*, Leipzig 1851 ; second edition, 1853 ; third edition, 1860 ; fourth edition, 1872.

[13] *Die Geschichtlichen Bücher des Alten Testaments*, Leipzig 1866.

[14] *Das Vorexilische Buch Israels und seine Erweiterungen*, Strassburg 1874.

[15] *Zeitschrift für Kirchliche Wissenschaft und Kirchliches Leben*, Leipzig 1880 ; cf. Delitzsch on "The Origin and Composition of the Pentateuch," in *The Presbyterian Review*, New York, pp. 553–558.

[16] Edinburgh.

CHAPTER IV.

DELITZSCH AS AUTHOR AND FRIEND OF AUTHORS.

"Wenn es überhaupt ein Surrogat für die Liebe gibt, so ist es
gewiss nur das Büchschreiben."—DELITZSCH.

IT is a wonder to any one who makes some computation of the work accomplished by Delitzsch where he got the time for all his varied occupations. We have seen that he rose at five o'clock in the morning the year around, and worked until late in the evening. He hardly ever took a vacation without having had an important interview with some learned man, or without visiting some library, or having secured some rare literary treasure.[1] His wife was called upon to make sacrifices in behalf of theological science, and to surrender hours to the learned world which rightfully belonged to her.[2] And yet whether we contemplate him as lecturer and friend of students, or as author and friend of authors, or in his relations to God's covenant people, the monuments which he has left behind him in each department seem to bear this inscription, "This one thing I do."

He was richly endowed by nature and education

for the work of authorship. He was possessed of what is vulgarly called· genius, and also of the genius for work in an uncommon degree. Work was his life, and the hope of work his heaven.[3] He possessed no ordinary skill in the extremes of authorship. His essays on the Complutensian Poly-glott and others of a similar sort show the most exact investigation. Nor need we be surprised to find him writing sacred romances, based on the most careful investigations, but possessing all the charms of fiction.

Nor was he denied the joy of clearing up a mystery through the discovery of a manuscript. In finding the codex of Reuchlin he was enabled to establish the fact that the *textus receptus* of the New Testament ought to be supplanted by a critical text, since Erasmus had not only prepared it in a careless and slovenly way, but as his Greek manu-script did not contain a certain passage in Revelation, Delitzsch showed how he had supplemented his Greek text by translating from Latin into Greek.

Delitzsch was like an exquisite harp of many strings, and was possessed of a Semitic fancy which enabled him to travel through the Holy Land with-out ever having seen it, so that he could picture to himself Lake Genesseret.[4] He had a sympathetic power of imagination which at once made him a companion of David and Isaiah, and of Jesus Him-self. He could not only see them, but see with them.

He was a poet, hence to him the poetry of the Old Testament not merely consisted of so many pentametres, hexametres, etc. ; but it was music in his soul, which had passed far beyond the mere analysis.

As an expositor, therefore, he was not so much engaged in analysis, in counting and classifying the number of bones in the human anatomy of Scripture, but he was a divine painter, who often caught a seraphic vision. It may be that, like the works of the great masters, his paintings were not so exact in detail, but he sought to make them so. It is certainly a wonderful combination and variety which we find in his writings, and withal to the end a modesty and self-criticism which was equally wonderful [5]—a desire for accuracy and fidelity which ceased only with his last breath, an aspiration to give the very best from which all personal ambition to shine seemed to be banished. His life in relation to every department of his activity was the embodiment of the question with which he greeted his callers, *Womit kann ich Ihnen dienen?* "How can I serve you?" His literary performances are certainly open to criticism. The very opulence of his learning and the structure of his mind led him to strow treasures where they did not always belong ; but in judging of his performances we are not to contrast him with the ordinary interpreter who continues to analyse and dissect until nothing is left but dead men's bones. Each man has his mission, and

Delitzsch certainly had his.   Allusion has already been made to the pains which he took with his style in the preparation of his lectures, how in the earlier years certainly they were polished and elegant to the last degree.   A fine specimen of his style at the beginning of his career may be seen in one of his first articles, published in 1840.   In brilliancy of imagination and in literary finish it is an excellent performance for a young man of only twenty-seven.[6]

Not the least task which his biographer will have, will be to discover even the names of all the productions of his fertile pen.[7]

He began his literary career at the age of eighteen, and continued it fifty - nine years with increasing renown until after he was seventy-seven, within six days of the end.

His literary activity had its roots in his activity as Christian, as professor, as editor, and as the friend of Israel.   His Book for Communicants, as has been stated, was the precipitate of those precious hours of quiet devotion which he led for seven years.   In his commentaries on books of the Old and New Testaments, in his *Biblical Psychology*, his *System of Christian Apologetics*, and his *Messianic Prophecies*, we have the ripe fruits of his herculean and well-directed studies as *privat - docent* and professor for nearly forty-eight years; and in his lesser writings we see how the way was prepared in his capacity as editor and reviewer; and out of his love for Israel came the great work of his life, the translation of

the New Testament into Hebrew. All the while
he was an extensive reader. Nothing which had
any important bearing on his department escaped
him. In his biographical activity, and in another
sphere which I shall shortly mention, he saw into
more men's minds than perhaps any other scholar
living or dead. He read books as few do, and he
read men in the unpublished and published maiden
efforts of his pupils and friends which came under his
eye for suggestion or revision as perhaps no other.

He had a memory which is said to have retained
all that he had read for years. But he did not trust
to it alone. He never read anything which bore
upon his investigations without making a note of
it. He had his commentaries printed with wide
margins in quarto. They stood in one corner on
the upper shelf of his bookcase. If he found anything of importance, or which was interesting or
curious, he mounted his steps with the agility of
a young man, took down the appropriate volume,
wrote down the quotation, or any thought suggested
in reading, and at once returned the book to its
place. Is it any wonder that a man with such
habits was constantly rewriting his lectures, and
that his new editions were almost like new books?
He was wont to say that each had an individuality
of its own. He was not ever harping on the same
string or beating over old straw, but to the end of
life was acquiring new knowledge. Perhaps his
mode of making annotations gave opportunity for

references to the dissertations and works of his pupils. How many have smiled as they have found some quotations by this distinguished scholar from their maiden efforts.

One of his most remarkable traits was in his friendship for authors and publishers, both old and young.[8] He kept in most intimate connection with the heart of the learned world in his department. He knew personally or stood in correspondence with almost every Semitic scholar whose acquaintance was worth having, if he was inclined to be friendly, and sometimes worked in partnership with him.

As editor and friend of authors, no thief could have attempted to pick his pockets when he went out after dinner to a café without finding in one of them either proof or advance sheets. He read proof almost as if it were his only occupation. Authors, both old and young, in Germany, Switzerland, Scandinavia, Great Britain, and America, looked to him for criticism and suggestion. He was their trusted adviser as few would be, and stood in most intimate relations with publishers, especially regarding works bearing on the Old Testament. His recommendations commanded confidence on both sides.[9]

Think of a man, in addition to all his labours for others, who was editor-in-chief of two quarterly publications, — not to speak of his contributions to several periodicals and magazines, — of one for twenty-five years and of the other for fifteen, both of which he edited contemporaneously for eleven years.

It was perhaps because of the social element which was developed in him to a wonderful degree, as well as from his desire to help others, and to produce the very best result for the world of scholars, that he entered into so many partnerships in literary labour. One of his first joint literary efforts was in connection with Dr. Moritz Stein-schneider, who was then a fellow - student under Fleischer, and who is now the greatest living authority in Hebrew bibliography. He certainly received suggestions from all his literary friends, including even the youngest, but on the whole he gave far more than he received.

In the same way in which he loved to help forward his worthy students, he delighted to bring young and promising authors out of obscurity. He found Dr. Baer, then a Jewish pedagogue, who had laboured assiduously for twenty years in Massoretic text criticism, who was recognised by leading Jewish scholars as a man of great promise. He not only found him, but introduced him to Christian scholars, by superintending the publication of his *Texts of the Old Testament* (including the reading of the proof), to each of which he wrote learned prefaces, and also secured for him the degree of Doctor of Philosophy. His story of the discovery of Dr. Baer is as follows :—

"In the year 1852 there appeared a treatise written in Hebrew, of considerable size, concerning the accentual system of the then so-called metrical

books, entitled *Torath Emeth*, a companion piece to
the still unexcelled treatise of W. Heidenheim concerning the accentual system of the prose books,
which had appeared in the year 1808 with the title
Mischpete ha-teamim. The value of that treatise can
be estimated from the fact that S. D. Luzatto, professor in Padua, enriched it with contributions, and
J. M. Jost, the well-known writer, who died last year,
provided it with a preface. In this the testimonial
is given to the author, that with rare love and devotion, surrendering all reference to gain and a com-
fortable life, he had devoted himself to his science,
and that this writing, to which he had been compelled
to confine himself, was only a specimen of much
fruit of his unexampled industry. This preface not
only attracted my attention but also my sympathy.
I sought him in his retirement, and found my expec-
tations far exceeded. A Jewish elementary teacher
on small pay, he had gathered a rich library, and for
about twenty years had busied himself with Old
Testament critical studies, which had cost him not a
little, and brought him in absolutely nothing. Un-
assuming, without the gift of making himself known,
loving science connected with the Old Testament
word of God, he offered the marrow of his youth to
the criticism of the Hebrew text, and secured a
knowledge of the Massora, including the oldest
national grammarians, which neither under Jewish
nor under Christian investigations has its equal." [10]

He considered it a praiseworthy attempt to draw

E

forth the studies of this learned man to the light. The sequel is well known to Old Testament scholars.

He read all the proofs of Fürst's *Concordance* [11] before he was twenty-seven years old, besides, doubtless, furnishing the Latin definitions and the preface. If any one wishes to get an impression of the magnitude of the undertaking, let him examine this Concordance. His services in all these directions were not slight; whatever he did, he did with his whole heart.

He made important contributions to Gesenius' *Lexicon*, edited by Mühlau and Volck, and read all the proofs. [12]

Indeed, it would be almost safe to say that no important work was published on the Old Testament in Leipzig which did not come, more or less, under his eye and hand.

He revised Biesenthal's *Commentary on the Hebrews*, and read all the proofs. [13] He was also instrumental in securing the degree of Doctor of Divinity from the University of Giessen for his old friend. As Gregory and I had also had our share in the matter, we all three drove to Biesenthal's house on the occasion of his eightieth birthday to convey to him the joyful intelligence, and to present him with the diploma. Professor Delitzsch read to the old Jewish missionary of the London Society a beautiful address, engrossed with his own hand on paper with a silver border, in which he called him his beloved teacher. Biesenthal was completely overcome, and sobbed like a child.

Cheyne has mentioned Fleischer's contributions to his commentaries. They were of exceeding value. It was as great a pleasure to Fleischer to give them, as it was for Delitzsch to receive them. Without Delitzsch they would never have seen the light. It was a rare spectacle to see these two grey-headed men together in the simple study of the great Hebraist, their faces beaming with mutual affection and admiration, and their eyes flashing like rare gems from the Orient, as they discussed intricate points in Arabic grammar and etymology.

It was quite another scene when Professor Keil appeared, with whom Professor Delitzsch stood in close connection as author and collaborateur in the issue of the Old Testament series. Keil, dry and exact as his commentaries; Delitzsch, bright and animated: one representing the prose, and the other the poetry of exegesis.

Delitzsch never rested with a low ideal of authorship. Humbly recognising his faults, as we have seen, in an almost unexampled way to the very end, he sought perfection, even if it cost him his life.

NOTES.

[1] See Köhler, *Neue Kirchliche Zeitschrift*, Leipzig 1890, pp. 237, 238.

[2] See funeral address of Pastor Tranzschel, p. 29.

[3] Cf. *ibid.* p. 34.

[4] He told me once he had only to shut his eyes to see it.

[5] *Der Flügel des Engels*, Dresden 1840, p. iii.: "Finally, I beg the reader to overlook many hard and obscure things in my manner of writing. I know that the highest simplicity of style is at the same time the highest beauty, and that through wise and beautiful words the cross of Christ may be made of none effect. How gladly I would understand how to learn to speak the simple, modest, and chaste language of wisdom from above. I perceive, with great mortification, that I am yet very far from the goal of my effort."

In the preface to the last edition of his *Commentary on Isaiah*, Leipzig 1889, he says: "Complaint has been made against my commentary, in its earlier editions, that it contains too much that is etymological, and too much that is curious, which is remote from an exegetical work. The reproach was not unjustified, and I have taken pains that it cannot be raised against the commentary in its new form.

[6] Rudelbach und Guericke, *Zeitschrift für die Gesammte Lutherische Theologie und Kirche*, Leipzig 1840. In the first issue of this Review is an article by Delitzsch on "Unglaube, Glaube, Neuglaube, Ein Beitrag zur Christlichen Psychologie," pp. 70–105.

[7] See Appendix III.

[8] An affectionate correspondence was kept up by him until his death with the junior partner of the firm who publish this work, resulting from the kindly friendship formed in the early youth of the latter when he was connected with a publishing house in Leipzig.

[9] He was the one who, with the approval of Professor Luthardt, recommended Mr. Caspar René Gregory to the J. C. Hinrichs'sche Buchhandlung as the proper person to prepare the Prolegomena to the eighth edition of Tischendorf's Greek Testament.

[10] *Zeitschrift für die Gesammte Lutherische Theologie*, Leipzig 1863, pp. 409 ff.

[11] *Librorum Sacrorum Veteris Testamenti Concordantiae Hebraicae atque Chaldaicae*, Lipsiae, p. xii.

[12] See *Vorwort zur neunten Auflage*, Leipzig 1883, p. v.

[13] See *Das Trostschreiben des Apostels Paulus an die Hebräer, kritisch wiederhergestellt und sprachlich, archäologisch und biblisch-theologisch erläutert*, Leipzig 1878, p. x.

CHAPTER V

DELITZSCH AS THE FRIEND OF ISRAEL.

"Und wenn es mein Leben kosten sollte die Arbeit am Neuen
Testament muss gethan werden."—DELITZSCH.

DELITZSCH never forgot the debt which he owed
to his benefactor.   He was not only accustomed to visit his grave and adorn it with flowers
when he came to Leipzig from Rostock and Erlangen,
but while his foster-father lived he found an inspiration and object in his efforts for the Jews in seeking
the conversion of Hirsch.   So far as I know, he was
his first convert.

Delitzsch never ceased to love Israel.   This is
evident from the whole tenor of his life.   The
teacher whom he esteemed most as a young man,
and for whom he took the lance, was the Jewish
scholar Julius Fürst.   His maiden effort, so far as I
am aware, in book-making—not to mention some
pamphlets—was a learned treatise on the "History
of Jewish Poetry, from the conclusion of the Holy
Scriptures of the Old Covenant until the most
recent times," in which he mentions over four
hundred Jewish poets and poems.   If he read these

in the most superficial way, this would be a remarkable performance for a young man of twenty-three; but it bears marks of careful reading and study.

The most cherished companion of his student days in the university, with whom he says he lived like a dove in one nest, was C. P. Caspari, now professor in Christiania. His first *famulus*, as has been remarked, was also a Jewish proselyte, Bernhard Caspari, brother of the one just mentioned.

His purse was ever open to the poor outcast Jew. None that was worthy ever sought his help in vain. It is certain that not a few who were unworthy enjoyed his bounty. For twenty-five years he conducted a magazine in the interest of Jewish missions. Within the last decade, when fanaticism was at white heat, and it was not popular to be a friend of the Jews, he entered the lists in their behalf with all the treasures of his Talmudical learning and an eloquence born of love. The literary work on which he spent nearly fifty years of study, which has passed through ten editions, and has had a circulation of 60,000, was the New Testament translated into Hebrew. The two works which especially engaged his attention during his last illness were the *Messianic Prophecies*, which was published in the interest of Jewish Missions, and the eleventh edition of his New Testament, which he hoped to be able to complete, even if his life were to be shortened by the effort. The two who had ready access to him during his last illness were the Jewish missionary, Pastor Wilhelm Faber, whom he wished to see daily to learn about the progress of the *Institutum Judaicum* and any items of interest in the Jewish work, and Lic. theol. Dr. Dalman, editor of the Hebrew New Testament. The last proof that he ever read was half of the first revised sheet of the New Testament. Surely these facts show where his heart was. And Faber well says: "Our glorified father and friend now raises his hands in prayer in the triumphant Church. We of the militant Church are sure of the blessing which will go forth upon those who are contending for Israel's salvation."

Prof. Delitzsch first received his introduction to Jewish missions through the missionaries Becker and Goldberg, who were wont to visit the fairs in Leipzig, where many Jews were accustomed to congregate. But while the flame of love burned ever brightly in his own heart, Jewish missions suffered a decline in the Lutheran Church. In order to kindle these dying embers into a flame, he founded " *Sown in Hope*, a magazine for the mission of the Church to Israel, issued in quarterly numbers by Professor Delitzsch and Pastor Becker. First number (Johannis, 1863).[1] Organ of the Evangelical Lutheran Missionary Society for Israel in Saxony and Bavaria." For twenty-five years he devoted time without stint in preparing articles for this magazine and in editing it. His spirit may be seen from the preface to the first number: "But we are persuaded that not a single word of prayer for Israel is in vain, but will have its part in filling up the chasm [between the Church and the Synagogue]. Therefore we sow in hope, and water our seed with our tears; and even though the black earth swallows our grain, yet the indwelling power of the Divine promise will not be in vain. 'Behold, the husbandman,' says James (v. 7), who has prayed for his people so earnestly that his knees have become horny, 'waiteth for the precious fruit of the earth, being patient over it, until it receives the early and the latter rain.' The early rain, that it may moisten the seed, and the latter rain, that it may ripen the heads we commit to Him who has promised it, and are content to prepare the way for the fulfilment of the promise to a certain degree through our sowing. Although the soil may be so barren, we hope against hope. Our hope rests in God's promise (Isa. xxvii. 6): 'It will at length come to pass that Jacob shall strike root, and Israel shall blossom and become green, that they may fill the earth with fruit.' "

As early as 1838, in his treatise entitled *Science, Art, Judaism*,[2] he expressed the opinion that the Hebrew version of the New Testament, published by the London Missionary Society, was only imperfectly adapted to the purposes of missions. There were mistakes in the titles of single books. He says, "Therefore, even at that time, I entertained the plan of undertaking the work, and, if possible, of producing something more thorough. . . .

In the translation of the apostolic hymn on love
(1 Cor. xiii.), I gave a specimen."

He did not undertake this version in any contro-
versial spirit, for he writes : " We shall work for that
which is best, but in quiet, and with the constant
wish for peaceful co-operation with all the friends of
our missionary cause." [3]

In 1865 he reports that "the work of translating
the New Testament into Hebrew is making constant
progress. . . . The translation of Matthew, of the
Epistle of James, the Epistle to the Hebrews, and
the Revelation—since these books were to be undertaken first according to our programme—has been
finished, and there is only lacking the final revision
and polishing. If the honourable committee of the
society, whose co-operation we need, do not become
weary, it might be possible to extend the work of
translation further to all the New Testament books,
and perhaps to publish the whole in the course of a
year. The undersigned entertains the hope that he
may be permitted to survive the conclusion of this
work, which is of the highest importance for the
cause of missions, and also for science." [4]

At the annual meeting of the Central Society
for Missions among the Jews, held in Leipzig, May
28th, 1874, it was reported: " The translation of the
New Testament into Hebrew is ready for the press,
and before it is given to the printers, only needs
a final revision by Professor Delitzsch, who intends
to devote the year 1875 entirely to the labour of

printing this work.   As programme, and at the same time example, of this new translation, he issued in the year 1870 the Epistle to the Romans.[5]   The firm of Dörffling and Franke has undertaken the publication."

The history of this translation for the next three years cannot be distinctly traced.   It is the recollection of Professor Caspar René Gregory, who composed the letters to the British and Foreign Bible Society, that Professor Delitzsch had entered into a verbal understanding with Perthes, the publisher at Gotha, during his visit to the Spring Fair in Leipzig 1875.

Gregory dissuaded Delitzsch, who had been unsuccessful in his correspondence with the British and Foreign Bible Society, from giving the Hebrew New Testament into the hands of an individual publisher, as, in that case, the circulation would be only limited.   He himself undertook the necessary correspondence, determining the form of the letters (which were signed by Delitzsch), with happy results, as the negotiations were completely successful.   Thus Professor Gregory was directly instrumental in securing a much wider circulation than would otherwise have been possible.   I now give the narrative as it was written by Professor Delitzsch himself, in English.   I was quite familiar at the time with the efforts which he made to secure a perfect translation.

" Many years I sought for a publisher of the whole, who would take upon himself the expense of publishing, and provide for its circulation.   At last

the British and Foreign Bible Society lent me its
helpful hand, and having obtained such a powerful
and generous protection, the new translation went
through the press, and forthwith enjoyed God's
wonderful blessing. It was completed in the spring
of 1877. The text followed there is substantially
that of the Sinaitic codex, with the principal
variations of the *textus receptus* in brackets. But
I soon felt that a text formed by myself alone could
not be exempt from individual arbitrariness, and that
it was more natural to base the translation on the
receptus and to supplement it with critical remarks.
After half a year a second edition became necessary,
which I based on these principles; it bears the date
of 1878. Only two years later, in 1880, a third
edition appeared in a larger form. Even the copies
of this third were quickly exhausted, and already, in
October of the same year, I prepared, at Berlin, with
my never-to-be-forgotten friend the late Rev. Palmer
Davies, a fourth electrotyped edition. The text
had now to be definitively settled, and the work
demanded redoubled care. I revised it a third time,
and was successfully aided by the Rev. T. R. Driver,
now Pusey's successor as Professor of Hebrew at
Oxford. Each of these editions represents, as I
hope, a new degree of approximation to the ideal,
which even now, in the fourth electrotyped edition
of 1882, is still not attained. Therefore, I was
agreeably surprised when Mr. James Watt, the
successor of the late Mr. Davies, informed me that

five thousand copies of the fourth edition were
sold, without any remaining. In truth, God has
abundantly blessed our work. Far from priding
myself, I acknowledge, on the contrary, the merits
of my fellow - labourers, among whom are also
not a small number of Jewish friends. We have
cause to say, that our new translation has contributed somewhat to bring the New Testament
nearer to the Jews, as a prominent work of their
literature." [6]

I now pass over several years, to the last that he
ever wrote on this subject :—

"The older I became, the more it seemed to me a
duty to give my scientific labours, as far as possible,
a practical aim. And in the great vineyard of God
it was the mission among Israel, the winning of
the Jewish people for Christianity, which attracted
me most. Therefore I was inspired with zeal to
co-operate in the building up of the new missionary
literature which was called into life by our Leipzig
Institutum Judaicum. But, since 1886, the main
contribution with which I wished to close my life,
was the completion of a fresh revision of the Hebrew
New Testament more thorough and complete than
ever before, corresponding to the high ideal which
I had placed before me,—a final edition, the utmost
which my intellectual power and length of life would
permit. After describing his physical condition, he
says, "What will be the end ? Will God make me
riper for eternity through a long mortal confinement

to my bed, or does He intend to remove me suddenly through the gates of death, or does He propose to give me a little season for convalesence ? I do not yet know to-day, the 29th of January 1890, but I owe Him unceasing thanks, that He has hitherto preserved my mind clear and fresh, and not only desirous of work, but also, although in a limited way, capable of work ; and to what task should I devote the remnant of my life and power of work as an offering beside the one I have indicated above, as the ideal aim of my life ? "

It remains briefly to add a quotation from a letter received from Dr. Dalman. " It was the most ardent wish of his heart, without a doubt, to finish the revision of the New Testament, for which he had made preparations, as the keystone of more than fifty years' labour. But at the end of January, as the firm which had been engaged to undertake the publication pressed to make a beginning, he saw that he must sacrifice this wish so natural to the decree of God. Those who know with what peculiar pains he was accustomed to watch the printing of his publications can form some conception of what it cost him to see others take his place, even if he had been permitted to survive the completion of the work. He asked me whether I was ready, with the aid of the Jewish savant, Israel Isar Kahan, who since 1883 had gone hand in hand with him in the revision and correction of the editions of the Hebrew New Testament which had appeared since

that time, to make the revision, which he had prepared, ready for the printer, and to carry it through
the press. After I had given my consent, although
not without hesitation, he gave me his own copy,
provided with a great quantity of notes; and then
began through the last month of his life continual
conferences, in which I had opportunity to obtain
from him in the preparation of the Gospel of
Matthew, which I had taken in hand, his directions
and wishes in doubtful cases, and also to establish
for this work the principles of procedure. To this
activity he devoted his last strength. Here he did
not spare himself. He turned aside entreaties that
he would not over-exert himself, and that he would
remember the sleepless nights which were occasioned
by the revision, with the brief words: 'And if it
should cost me my life, the work on the New Testament must be done.' Every other consideration
had to give way. Meanwhile the printing had
begun. On the evening of the 1st of March I was
able to give him half of the first proof sheet. The
following day—the last Sunday that he lived, and
the last day of completely undisturbed consciousness
—these were the leaves which he took again and
again in hand, which he read again and again, and
which, finally, he handed back to me with a remark
concerning the grammatical contents, which he
himself had written on the margin. To see this
work really in progress was his last pleasure; the
examination of its leaves the last work of this

unwearied man, who now lay with waning spirit and waning body on his death-bed."

The end has already been described in the sketch of his life ; but it is evident that his last illness and his dying hours were devoted to the people whom he loved, for whom he had prayed, and to whom he had consecrated some of the best energies of his life. May this love and devotion not be lost in the days to come.

NOTES.

[1] *Saat auf Hoffnung. Zeitschrift für die Mission der Kirche an Israel*, etc., Leipzig 1863.

[2] See Appendix III.

[3] *Saat auf Hoffnung*, Leipzig 1864, part iii. pp. 59–62. *Studien und Kritiken*, Gotha 1865, pp. 611–614.

[4] *Saat auf Hoffnung*, Leipzig 1865, part i. pp. 61, 62.

[5] *Paulus des Apostles Brief an die Römer aus dem Griechischen Urtext auf Grund des Sinai-Codex in das Hebräische übersetz und aus Talmud und Midrasch erläutert von Franz Delitzsch* [*Mit einem Rückblick auf die Uebersetzungsgeschichte vom ersten bis ins neunzehnte Jahrhundert*], Leipzig 1870.

[6] *The Hebrew New Testament of the British and Foreign Bible Society:* A contribution to Hebrew Philology, Leipzig 1883.

APPENDIX.

——o——

I.

Franciscvs Ivlivs Delitzsch.

Hic a xiii. Lipsiae natus Jo. Godofredo, scrutario, ex Io. Rosina Mueleria, hominis Judaei beneficio nutritus et educatus est. Ludo primum privato, deinde in schola senatoria puerili disciplina instructus, semestrique institutione gratuita Weigelii, olim quarti scholae Thomanae magistri, praeparatus, in tertiam classem scholae ad D. Nicolai est receptus. Postremo vitae scholasticae tempore furore poetico correptus carmen edidit hoc titulo: Ein Lied von dem Einen, das noth ist; quod nunc palam detestatur. Quum in Academiam discessisset, Richteri scholis ad philosophiam excitatus, Fichtii idealismus amplexus est, quumque in pulchri naturam inquiriret, delatus ad mathesin, spe inveniendae curvae Hogarthianae. Is aestus ubi deferbuit, a xxxii. se theologiae applicuit, litterisque potissimum Thalmudicis operam dans, duce Julio Fuerstio, homine ingenio doctrinaque mirabili, nuper ab Senatu urbis nostris ampl. interpres scriptionum Judicarum est constitutus, pp. 29–30.

Panegyrici magistri, Lips. 1826–50.
D.V. Martii A. MDCCCXXXV.
Lipsiae.

F

II.

AUTOBIOGRAPHY.[1]

I was born in Leipzig, the 23rd of February 1813, and was baptized the 4th of March in the Nicolai Church. My father, who was from Leisnig,[2] had at that time, and during my childhood, a business in old things, a so-called merchandise booth. He lived in straitened circumstances, and I had a hard youth. My father died the 4th of April 1836, in the fifty-fourth year of his age.

My benefactor from my youth was a Jew named Levy Hirsch. He lived with us in one house, and dealt in books. Without him I should never have been able to enter upon a course of study. First I attended a school for boys, and was later received into the city free school, in which Plato was then rector, and Dolz vice-rector. Here I became a complete Rationalist. I indeed felt an ardent desire for God; but the person of the Saviour was veiled for me in thick darkness. At the university I studied first philology and philosophy. Longing for truth, I buried myself in the systems of the great German philosophers. Fichte especially attracted me.

One of my university friends, named Schütz, laboured unceasingly to bring me to belief. I resisted a long time. But even now I can point out the place upon one of the streets of Leipzig [not far from the former Grimma Gate in the Goethe Street, near the corner of Grimma Street] where a flash from above placed me in the condition in which

---

[1] This first appeared in the Norwegian *Missions Blad for Israel*, 1883, p. 51 ff. My translation was made from the German rendering prepared by Pastor Wilhelm Faber, which appeared in *Saat auf Hoffnung*, Leipzig 1890, pp. 147–151. An English translation of the Norwegian was given by Professor Hilprecht in the *Old Testament Student*, 1887, p. 209 ff.

[2] Not Leipzig, which is certainly a typographical error.

Thomas found himself when he cried, "My Lord and my God!" Henceforth I became a theologian. I sought intercourse with students who were awakened through God's grace, and cultivated the acquaintance of believing family circles in Leipzig. The years 1832–1834, my last years at the university, were the most beautiful in my life. They were the days of my first love, the spring-time of my temporal life.

I came into communication with the Jewish missionaries Goldberg and Becker, who visited the fairs at Leipzig in order to work among the Jews. Both these men first taught me to love the people from whom the Saviour sprang according to the flesh, and taught me to pray for their conversion to the Christ whom they had rejected.

Now, when they call me a celebrated Hebraist, it sounds almost strange that missionary Becker gave me the first instruction in Rabbinical Hebrew; but so it is. I had brought some knowledge of Hebrew with me from the gymnasium, and this language was my favourite study. I made the beginning in Rabbinical Hebrew with the treatise, *Or leeth ereb*, "Light at Evening," which missionary Becker read with me.

One object of my missionary activity was my benefactor Hirsch. My testimony concerning Christ to him brought forth late, but ripe fruit. On the 10th of May 1843 my beloved benefactor was baptized. Two years later he went home in peace.

For seven years, 1835–1842, I led the devotional meetings in a circle of believing friends. Some of the members still live, and when we meet we confess that our anchor still rests upon the old ground. Employed in this practical way, I devoted myself on the other hand entirely to Hebrew and Old Testament studies. These led me to the school of Rosenmüller, where I was brought into connection with Fleischer and my dear Paul Caspari. Our aim was the same; and although we were very different, we loved each other, and were very intimate. Now, when I see my friend among the representatives of the Norwegian Church and Mission, I praise God's gracious guidance.

I have not yet mentioned my mother. She was the daughter of a musician, in a little town between Leipzig and Halle. As she became a widow, and was alone in the world, she managed a small business in books; and when I was professor my mother was still engaged in the sale of old books. This contrast grieved me very much; but she desired to be independent, and no one could blame her for that. She was a good woman, respected and beloved by all who knew her. She had little pleasure in this world. When she died in my arms, December 17th, 1857, she was glad to be able to go home. I am not the only one who visits her grave from time to time. She was a true cross-bearer, to whom Luke vii. 47 well applies.

I have been asked many times for a sketch of my life. I have never been so communicative before as now to my Norwegian brethren.

My later life and activity is quickly described. In the year 1842 I received permission to lecture in Leipzig by means of a treatise on the Prophet Habakkuk. My *Communion Book* originated in the meetings for edification which I held. In my youthful enthusiasm for Jewish literature, I wrote my book on the History of post-Biblical Jewish Poetry. In the year 1846 I became a professor in Rostock, in 1850 in Erlangen, and in 1867 in Leipzig, where I hope to remain until my blessed end. In Erlangen I founded, in the year 1863, in connection with the Bavarian Jewish Mission, the missionary magazine, *Saat auf Hoffnung* (Sown in Hope). My Hebrew New Testament, which first appeared in 1877, is now being printed in the fifth edition. I am not least indebted to the generosity of the Norwegian brethren, who have made the issue of this work possible.

I became acquainted with my wife through our devotional meetings. Her mother and her brother confessed Christ. We were married April 27th, 1845.

The fruit of this union was four sons. The eldest, Johannes, died as a professor *extraordinarius* of theology, February 3rd, 1876, just as he had finished editing Oehler's *Symbolik*. He found his resting-place in the Evangelical Churchyard at Genoa. On the 17th of January 1872 his brother Ernst had already gone home. As assistant-surgeon he had participated in the Franco-German war from beginning to end. Not until long after the conclusion of peace was he able to come home. After he had been sickly for quite awhile, he fell a prey to acute pneumonia. His grave is in Leipzig. My two youngest sons are still alive. The elder of them, Hermann, has a position in the Allegemeinen Deutschen Credit Bank, and the younger, Friedrich, born September 3rd, 1850, is professor *extraordinarius* of Assyriology, and is now engaged at the British Museum of London, where he continues his studies preparatory to the issue of a Babylonio-Assyrian Lexicon.

On the 23rd of February I completed my seventieth year. Although I hate all ovations, I had more than I like. Many congratulations, especially outside of Germany, were sent me, which I received so gladly, and they sounded so sweetly in my ears, as sweetly as the lullaby sounds to the child when it is rocked to sleep.

III.

PARTIAL LIST OF BOOKS AND PAMPHLETS BY PROFESSOR DELITZSCH.

NOTE.— * *Designates such books by Delitzsch as I have not seen.*

1831.

1. *Ein Lied von dem Einen, das noth ist, gesungen all seinen deutschen Brüdern, insonderheit seiner

lieben Burschenschaft, Leipzig 1831. Cf. the contemptuous reference to it in his Vita.

1836.

2. Zur Geschichte der jüdischen Poësie vom Abschluss der heiligen Schriften Alten Bundes bis auf die neueste Zeit von Franz Delitzsch, Leipzig 1836. Preface dated May 1st, hence the work which mentions over four hundred and fifty Jewish poets and poems was prepared before he was twenty-three years old.

1838.

3. Wissenschaft, Kunst, Judenthum. Schilderungen und Kritiken von Franz Delitzsch, Grimma 1838. This is the book in which he gives a specimen of a new translation of the New Testament in his rendering of 1 Cor. xiii.

4. Iesurun sive Prolegomenon in Concordantias Veteris Testamenti a Julio Fuerstio editas Libri Tres, auctore Francisco Delitzschio, Grimmae 1838. Dedicated to Fuerst. This is a wonderfully learned work for a young man of twenty-five, in which he treats: (Book I.) of the history of the Hebrew language from Origen to Fürst; (Book II.) the origin, nature, and dignity of the language; (Book III.) the excellence of the Sanscrit language. Fürst was unjust enough to write concerning this book in his Bibliotheca Judaica, Leipzig 1849-51, i. p. 204: "ausgezogen aus dem Concordanz," "taken from the Concordance." Steinschneider, in his Bibliographisches Handbuch, Leipzig 1859, p. 40, remarks that Delitzsch considered himself as a collaborator on the Concordance, and Fürst devotes about half of the preface of the Concordance to a description and praise of Delitzsch's "Prolegomenon," and concludes with the following acknowledgment: "Hoc voto dum concludo et ita peroro, non possum, quin publice gratum meum animum

testificer *Fr. Delitzschio*, Phil. Dr., adolescenti doctrina disciplinaque praestantissimo, cujus vivo literarum amore et adjutrice consuetudine non paucae de disquisitionibus meis interioribus ac reconditis matureront. Praeclara ejus in literis biblicis ac judaicis eruditio, quam jam compluribus operibus satis luculente comprobavit, eum, quamquam in rebus theologicis prorsus a me dissentientem, socium atque adjutorum mihi adjunxit, quem in literis rabbinicis ac talmudicis antea auditorem et discipulum habuisse merito glorior. Quantum se in mentem meam insinuaverit, quanta sagacitate in intimos disciplinae meae recessus penetraverit, quam prospere progressus meos non solum persecutus fuerit, sed etiam promovere studuerit, testantur ejus in has Concordantias *Prolegomena*. Huic igitur me plus, quam correctori acceptum referre fateor; huic in hoc ipso maximo industriae doctrinaeque meae opere quod ad posteros perventurum spero, meritas debitasque gratias, tanquam praemium voluntate mea multo minus publice persolvo.

1839.

5. Luthenthum und Lügenthum. Ein offenes Bekentniss beim Reformationsjubiläum der Stadt Leipzig, Grimma 1839. A plea for strict and genuine Lutheranism.

1840.

6. Der Flügel des Engels. Eine Stimme aus der Wüste im vierten Jubel-Fest-Jahre der Buchdruckerkunst, Dresden 1840. Maintains that the Lutheran Church should have a part in the celebration of this festival. "It should not appear as if its belief had become old, its confession dumb, and that its literary and symbolical confessors have died out." In this book he begs the reader to overlook many obscure things in his manner of writing.

1841.

7. פצעי אוהב* Eine Missionsrede, mit Bezugnahme auf die Judenverfolgungen zu Damaskus und Rhodus, gehalten Dresden 1841.

8. Anekdota zur Geschichte der mittelalterlichen Scholastik unter Juden und Moslemen aus hebräischen und arabischen Handschriften der Stadt und Universitätsbibliothek zu Leipzig, der Königlichen Bibliotheken zu Dresden und München und der Waisenhausbibliothek zu Halle, Leipzig 1841.

He found the MS. on which the book was based as he catalogued the Hebrew MSS. of the city library of Leipzig in 1837. He was aided in the work by a young Jewish scholar, Moritz Steinschneider, and also by his teacher, Professor Fleischer. After fifty pages of Prolegomena, the rest is in Hebrew, except twenty-seven pages of Arabic, etc.

9. Philemon oder das Buch von der Freundschaft in Christo. Den zerstreuten Bekennern des Herrn zur Belebung und Regelung ihrer Gemeinschaft gewidmet, [" Aufzeichnungen der Fräulein S. C. von Klettenberg und ihres Freundes Kreises "], Leipzig 1841; third ed. Gotha 1878.

1842.

10. Schatzkästlein geistlicher Sinngedichte und Reimsprüche auf alle Tage des Jahres zur Erweckung, Uebung und Förderung des mit Christo in Gott verborgenen Lebens. Gesammelt, angeordnet und bevorwortet von Franz Delitzsch, Dresden 1842.

11. Wer Sind die Mystiker? Eine gründliche Belehrung über das was Mysticismus ist und nicht ist. Gegen die Sprachverwirrung unserer Zeit, Leipzig 1842.

12. De Habacuci Prophaetae, etc. Editio auctior et emendatior, Lipsiae 1842.

1843.

13. Der Prophet Habakuk, ausgelegt, Leipzig 1843.

This was based on his studies in connection with his dissertation, which was presented to the Theological Faculty of Leipzig the preceding year, that he might obtain permission to lecture, and which was entitled: " De Habacuci Prophaetae Vita atque Aetate."

1844.

14. Das Sacrament des wahren Leibes und Blutes Jesu Christi. Beicht- und Communion-Gebete von Franz Delitzsch, Doctor der Philosophie, Licentiat und Privatdocent der Theologie zu Leipzig, Dresden 1844. This is the book which Professor Luthardt says was specially blessed, and in which Delitzsch took almost more pleasure than in all his scientific works put together. The seventh edition appeared, Leipzig 1886.—Köhler.

1845.

15. Die biblische-prophetische Theologie, ihre Fortbildung durch Chr. A. Crusius und ihre neueste Entwickelung seit der Christologie Hengstenbergs. Historisch - Kritisch dargestellt, Leipzig 1845. An important work for the literature of Old Testament Theology.

1846.

16. Symbolae ad Psalmos illustrandos isagogicae. Disseritur I. de Psalmorum indole partim jehovica partim elohimica; II. de Psalmorum ordine ejusque causis ac legibus, Lipsiae 1846.

1847.

17. Vier Bücher von der Kirche. Seitenstück zu Löhe's drei Büchern von der Kirche, Dresden 1847. Dedicated to the Theological Faculty of Erlangen in recognition of the degree of Doctor of Divinity which had been conferred by them upon him.

1849.

18. * Vom Hause Gottes oder der Kirche. Katechismus in drei Hauptstücken, Dresden 1849. "The evangelical independence with which the official arrangements of the Apostolic Church are represented, according to their very differing value for the kingdom of God, and which are declared not to be a 'binding law,' stands in edifying contrast with the new Popish zeal of many Protestant contemporaries who seek to *apostolise* the head and hair, but not the flesh and blood of Christianity."—Ströbel.

1851.

19. Das Hohelied untersucht und ausgelegt, Leipzig 1851. Maintains that it is a drama in six acts, and that the idea of marriage is that of Canticles, and hence that the mystery of marriage is its mystery.

1852.

20. * Die bayerische Abendmahlsgemeinschaftsfrage, Erlangen 1852.

21. Die Genesis ausgelegt von Franz Delitzsch, Leipzig 1852. Maintains that there are two documents in the Pentateuch, which are to be distinguished by the use of the divine names: the one is Mosaic, the other is from the time of Joshua. Second edition, 1853; third, 1868; fourth, 1872.

22. * Anweisung zu heilsamen Lesen der heiligen Schrift. Sieben Regeln gepredigt am siebenten Sonntag nach Trinitatis, 1852 [Jahrestag der Erlanger Bibelgesellschaft], Erlangen 1852.

1853.

23. Neue Untersuchungen über Entstehung und Anlage der kanonischen Evangelien, Erster Theil. Das Mattheus Evangelium, Leipzig 1853.

24. * Das Gebet und die Heidenmission. Predigt über Luc. vi. 12, 13 gehalten am Missionsfest in Nürnberg den 21 Juni 1853, Nürnberg 1853.

1855.

25. System der Biblischen Psychologie, Leipzig 1855; second ed. 1861. A System of Biblical Psychology, Edinburgh, second English edition, 1879.

1857.

26. Commentar zum Briefe an die Hebräer mit Archäologischen und Dogmatischen Excursen über das Oper und die Versöhnung. Commentary on the Epistle to the Hebrews, Edinburgh, vol. i. 1868; vol. ii. 1870.

1859–1860.

27. Die Akademische Amtstracht und ihre, Farben 1859.

28. Commentar über den Psalter. . . . Erster Theil. Uebersetzung und Auslegung von Psalm i.–lxxxix., Leipzig 1859. Zweiter Theil. Uebersetzung und Auslegung von Psalm xc.–cl. Nebst der Einleitung in den Psalter und vielen Beilagen massorethischen und accentuologischen Inhalts, Leipzig 1860; second ed. 1867; third ed. 1873–74; fourth ed. 1883. Biblical Commentary on the Psalms, vols. i.–iii., Edinburgh 1871. Translated from the second German edition. Also a translation of the fourth edition, vols. i.–iii., London 1887–89.

1861.

29. Handschriftliche Funde. . . . Erstes Heft : Die Erasmischen Entstellungen des Textes der Apokalypse, Nachgewiesen aus dem Verloren Geglaubten Codex Reuchlins. In connection with his name as author of this work, all his titles are given, which is quite unusual. *Zweites Heft : Neue Studien über den Codex Reuchlin's und neue textgeschichtliche Aüfschlüsse über die Apocalypse. Mit Beiträgen von S. P. Tregelles. Year unknown.

1863.

30. * Für und wider Kahnis.

1864.

31. Biblischer Commentar über die poetischen
Bücher des Alten Testaments. II. Band: das Buch
Job, Leipzig 1864; second ed. 1876. Biblical Commentary on the Book of Job, first English ed. Edinburgh 1866; second English ed. 1868. New edition
in course of preparation, with many alterations and
additions by Professor Delitzsch. Practically a third
edition of the original, Edinburgh 1891.

1866.

32. Biblischer Commentar über den Prophet Jesaia.
Mit Beiträgen von Prof. Dr. Fleischer und Consul D.
Wetstein, Leipzig 1866; second ed. 1869; third ed.
1879; fourth ed. 1889. Biblical Commentary on the
Prophecies of Isaiah, Edinburgh 1873. From fourth
edition 1889, with additions and corrections by the
author, Edinburgh and New York 1890, 2 vols.

1867.

33. Jesus und Hilel. Mit Rüsicht auf Renan und
Geiger verglichen von Franz Delitzsch. 2te revid.
Auflage, Erlangen 1867; third ed. 1879.

1868.

34. Physiologie und Musik in ihrer Bedeutung für
die Grammatik, besonders die hebräische. Eine
akademische Rede. Mit drei physikalischen Abbil-
ungen und einem musikalischem Beilage, Leipzig.

This treatise is of great interest, because some of
those who were opposed to the call of Professor
Delitzsch to Leipzig urged against him that he did
not possess a knowledge of Hebrew grammar that
was sufficiently thorough. He chose, however, for his
inaugural address the subject named above, in which

he showed that notwithstanding the important contributions of Gesenius, Ewald, Hupfeld, and Olshausen, there were many questions concerning which the grammarians indicated gave no satisfactory answers.

Dr. Merkel, who was present when this address was delivered, testifies to the unusual impression which was made by it. Zeitschrift für die gesammte lutherische Theologie und Kirche, Leipzig 1869, p. 283.

35. Handwerkerleben zur Zeit Jesu. Ein Beitrag zur neutestamentlichen Zeitgeschichte, Erlangen 1868 ; second ed. 1875 ; third ed. 1878. Jewish Artisan Life in the Time of our Lord, to which is appended a critical comparison between Jesus and Hillel, London 1877. Artisan Life, translated by Croll from the third ed., Philadelphia 1883, and by Pick, New York 1883. —Schaff.

1869.

36. System der christlichen Apologetik, Leipzig 1869.

1870.

37. Paulus des Apostels Brief an die Römer. Aus dem Griechischen Urtext auf Grund des Sinai Codex in das Hebräische übersetz und aus Talmud und Midrasch erläutert, Leipzig 1870.

1871.

38. Ein Tag in Capernaum erzählt, Leipzig 1871. Delitzsch says in the preface (p. 7), that he moved and lived in it half a year. He began to dictate it as he was deprived for some weeks of the use of his eyes. During the storms of war he found in it an asylum for his thoughts. Second ed. 1873.

39. Studien zur Entstehungsgeschichte der Polyglottenbibel des Cardinals Ximenes. Als akadem. Programm zur Reformationsfeier der Universität, Leipzig 1871.

1872.

40. Sehet welch ein Mensch! Ein Christusbild, Leipzig 1872.

1873.

41. Durch Krankheit zur Genesung. Eine jerusalemische Geschichte der Herodier - Zeit, Leipzig 1873.

In Nos. 38, 40, and 41, Professor Delitzsch gives examples of his power in basing romances upon his Talmudical and historical studies.

42. Das Salomonische Spruchbuch. Mit Beiträgen von Dr. Fleischer und Dr. Wetzstein, Leipzig 1873. Biblical Commentary on the Proverbs of Solomon, Edinburgh 1874.

1875.

43. Hoheslied und Koheleth, Leipzig 1875. He considers Ecclesiastes a post-Exilic book, one of the youngest in the Canon. Commentary on the Song of Songs and Ecclesiastes, Edinburgh 1877.

1877.

44. ספרי הברית החדשה נעתקים כליטֹן ין לֹליֹטֹן עברית בהשתדלות ובהשגחת החכם פראפעסאר פראנין דעליטֹש. Leipzig 1877. Ten editions have thus far appeared.

1878.

45. Complutensische Varianten zu dem alttestamentliche Texte, Leipzig 1878.

1880.

46. Messianic Prophecies. Lectures by Franz Delitzsch, Edinburgh 1880.

1881.

47. Old Testament History of Redemption. Lectures by Franz Delitzsch, Edinburgh 1881.

48. * Rohling's Talmudjude beleuchtet, 1881. Seven editions in one year.—Schaff.

1882.

49. Christenthum und jüdische Presse selbsterlebtes, Erlangen 1882. He says he has no sympathy for the anti-Semitic party. He does not discuss the Jewish press, but rather a Judaised Christian press.

1883.

50. * Was Dr. Rohling beschworen hat und noch beschwören will, Leipzig 1883.

51. The Hebrew New Testament of the British and Foreign Bible Society. A Contribution to Hebrew Philology, Leipzig 1883.

52. Schachmatt den Blutsügnern Rohling und Justus entboten, Erlangen 1883.

1885.

53. Die Bibel und der Wein, Leipzig 1885.

1887.

54. Neuer Commentar über die Genesis, Leipzig 1887. A New Commentary on Genesis, 2 vols., Edinburgh and New York 1889.

1888.

55. Iris, Farbenstudien und Blumenstücke, Leipzig 1888. Iris, Studies in Colour and Talks about Flowers, Edinburgh 1890.

1890.

56. Messianische Weissagungen in Geschichtlicher Folge, Leipzig 1890. Messianic Prophecies in Historical Succession, Edinburgh and New York 1891.

Year Unknown.

57. Jüdisch - Arabischer Poesien aus vormuhammedischer Zeit. Ein Specimen aus Fleischer's Schule, Leipzig.

No effort has been made to collect the titles of articles in Reviews. Professor Delitzsch himself gives a list of his Talmudical studies, which appeared in Guericke's Zeitschrift für die gesammte Lutherische Theologie und Kirche, Leipzig 1840–1878, in his appendix to "The Hebrew New Testament of the British and Foreign Bible Society," pp. 35, 36. He also refers, p. 37, to articles which appeared in Saat auf Hoffnung, and which have a bearing on his translation of the New Testament. Other articles were published in Luthardt's Zeitschrift für Kirchliche Wissenschaft und Kirchliches Leben, Leipzig 1880, etc., in Herzog and Plitt's Real-Encyklopädie, and in Riehm's Handwörterbuch. In recent years articles have been given to English readers in the Expositor and the Sunday School Times. No mention is made here of any of the works which he edited, as, for instance, the Hebrew texts, by Dr. Baer.

MORRISON AND GIBB, PRINTERS, EDINBURGH.

www.ingramcontent.com/pod-product-compliance
Lightning Source LLC
Chambersburg PA
CBHW020805020726
47495CB00008B/2601